MORE BONES

MORE

SCARY STORIES FROM

BONES

AROUND THE WORLD

Selected and Retold by
ARIELLE NORTH OLSON
and HOWARD SCHWARTZ

💀

Illustrated by E. M. GIST

VIKING

VIKING

Published by Penguin Group

Penguin Young Readers Group, 345 Hudson Street, New York, New York 10014, U.S.A.

Penguin Group (Canada), 90 Eglinton Avenue East, Suite 700, Toronto, Ontario, Canada M4P 2Y3

(a division of Pearson Penguin Canada Inc.)

Penguin Books Ltd, 80 Strand, London WC2R 0RL, England

Penguin Ireland, 25 St Stephen's Green, Dublin 2, Ireland (a division of Penguin Books Ltd)

Penguin Group (Australia), 250 Camberwell Road, Camberwell, Victoria 3124, Australia

(a division of Pearson Australia Group Pty Ltd)

Penguin Books India Pvt Ltd, 11 Community Centre, Panchsheel Park, New Delhi – 110 017, India

Penguin Group (NZ), 67 Apollo Drive, Rosedale, North Shore 0632, New Zealand

(a division of Pearson New Zealand Ltd)

Penguin Books (South Africa) (Pty) Ltd, 24 Sturdee Avenue, Rosebank, Johannesburg 2196, South Africa

Penguin Books Ltd, Registered Offices: 80 Strand, London WC2R 0RL, England

First published in 2008 by Viking, a division of Penguin Young Readers Group

1   3   5   7   9   10   8   6   4   2

LIBRARY OF CONGRESS CATALOGING-IN-PUBLICATION DATA IS AVAILABLE
ISBN 978-0-670-06339-0

Printed in the U.S.A.
Set in Goudy Old Style
Book design by Jim Hoover

For Randy and Melissa, Jens and Janet,
Laura, Eric, Miranda, and Rose
—with much love.
—A.N.Θ.

For Shira, Nati, Miriam, Ari, and Ava.
—H.S.

I would like to dedicate this book to Mom, Dad, Jeff,
and Krista, for all their support and guidance in life;
to Doug Stambaugh for all his help; to Meadow for more
love than one man deserves; but most importantly,
to the loving memory of Basil.
—E.M.G.

We would like to acknowledge the editors who contributed so much to this book: Tracy Gates, Kendra Levin, Harriet Sigerman, and Janet Pascal.

MORE BONES

CONTENTS

Introduction

The many readers of Ask the Bones have made their wishes clear—they want to hear bones rattle as soon as they open our books.

Take care if you read *More Bones* before you go to sleep. You don't want to wake up to find a draug staring at you, his head covered with seaweed and his teeth coated with green slime. If he invites you to take a boat ride with him—don't do it.

Beware of those lovely maidens who are not what they appear to be. Be especially careful of women who sharpen their teeth on wood or have beautiful red hair that turns into writhing serpents.

If you're reading these stories alone at night, watch out. When evil men need help carrying a corpse, they just might pick you for the job. And whatever you do, don't double-cross the witch who sleeps with a knife under her pillow.

We have dug deeply in every corner of the world—from Egypt to Iceland, from Japan to Germany, from Spain to Hawaii—for the scary stories in *More Bones*. Listen! Can you hear the bones beginning to rattle?

A Story to Tell
IRELAND

Pat Diver was not easily frightened. He had spent many lonely nights on the road traveling from one town to the next. But now a cold wind was whipping through the trees.

Pat trudged on, longing for a warm fire and a snug roof. He was a tinker who could repair a kettle or a saucepan in the wink of an eye. But no one wanted anything fixed in exchange for a night's lodging. "Go away," they said, even when Pat offered them a few coins.

He pulled his coat tightly across his chest and kept walking up the dark mountain road. Finally he came upon a cabin. When he looked through the window, he could see an old couple sitting beside a flickering fire. Surely they would welcome him.

The moment they opened the door, Pat asked if he could spend the night. He said he would pay them or mend their pots and pans. He would do anything for them, if only they would invite him inside.

The old man looked at the old woman and she nodded. "You can stay," he said, "if you tell us a story."

The tinker rubbed his cold hands together. "I wish I could," he said. "But I have no stories to tell."

"Not even one?" asked the old woman.

The tinker shook his head.

"Then be off!" the old man cried. "No one gets in here if he can't tell us a story." He slammed the door shut so quickly that the poor tinker stumbled backward and almost fell.

Pat didn't want to take another step. He was too tired, too cold, and angry besides. Never before had he encountered such unfriendly people.

He sneaked into the rickety old barn behind the cabin. There was a pile of straw in one corner. "Any bed will do," he muttered. He burrowed deeply into the straw, pulling it over himself until he was completely hidden from view. Within moments, he was sound asleep.

Later that night, harsh voices awakened him. He didn't dare make a sound, but he peeked through a little hole between some blades of straw. And there in the middle of the barn he saw two huge men starting a fire on the dirt floor. Their faces were almost hidden by their long, greasy hair. When the flames rose, Pat could see them pull something out from the shadows.

It was a corpse!

Pat could barely keep his teeth from chattering. He watched in horror as they tied a rope around its feet and hung it from a beam over the fire. Then one man turned it around and around, roasting it.

"I'm tired," the man said, "you take a turn."

"Not me," said the other. "Let Pat Diver turn it."

Pat gasped. How did they know he was there?

"Come on out," they shouted, kicking some straw aside.

What else could Pat do? He crawled out on his hands and knees. One man grabbed him by the scruff of his neck and set him on his feet.

"Start turning the corpse," said the other, "and mind you don't let it burn!"

Pat shuddered. His mouth went dry and sour. He thought he might faint, but the huge men bent down and glared at him just inches from his face. He had no choice. He gritted his teeth and turned that corpse as skillfully as a seasoned chef.

The huge men laughed at his terror. "Keep turning," one said.

"We'll be back," said the other, and they disappeared into the night.

Pat didn't dare to stop turning that corpse, even when the flames rose high around it. Before long, the flames reached the rope—quickly burning it. Pat watched in horror as the rope broke and the corpse fell into the fire. Sparks and ashes flew into the air.

And Pat? He flew out the door.

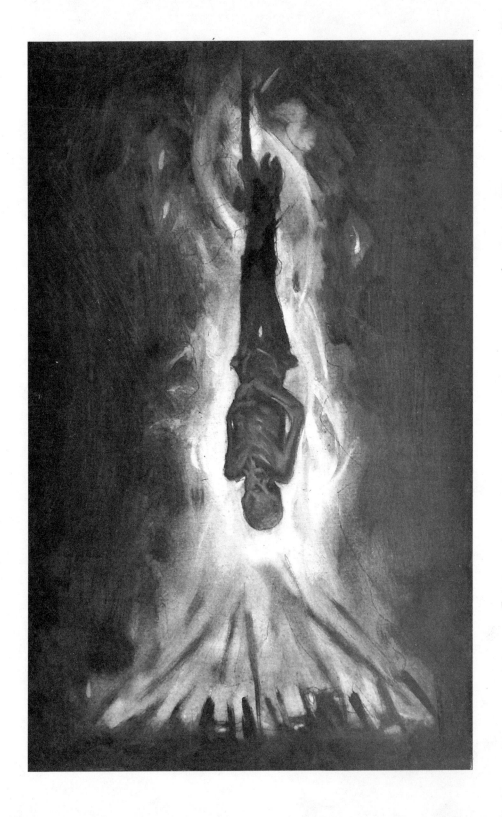

He ran faster than he had ever run in his entire life. He ran and ran and ran. Sweat poured down his face even though he was racing into a cold wind. His legs ached, but he wanted to put as much distance as he could between himself and those horrible men with the burning corpse.

When he couldn't run another step, he slid down into a soggy ditch and dove behind a clump of overgrown weeds. He hid there, panting. But he had barely caught his breath when he heard heavy footsteps coming down the road. Worse yet, he heard harsh voices. He peeked out and saw the same awful men he had seen in the barn.

"I'm tired of carrying this corpse," one man said. "You take a turn."

"Not me," said the other. "Let Pat Diver carry it," and he jumped into the ditch and dragged Pat out of the weeds.

Pat was already clammy and shivering, and when that smoky corpse was draped around his shoulders, his hair stood on end. He almost retched.

"It's your fault," one man said. "You're the one who burned it. Now we have to bury it."

"Move," said the other, and down that road they went— mile after mile. Pat thought his back was going to break. He desperately wanted to stop. He almost didn't care what those huge men did to him, but somehow he kept staggering along.

A sickle moon barely lit the way. Finally they reached an abandoned graveyard beside a tumbledown church. Weeds and vines and brambles covered the graves and broken walls. Owls hooted to one another, and bats circled low on silent wings.

The huge men shoved brambles aside. One grabbed a shovel and began digging a grave.

Pat let his awful burden slip quietly to the ground. He thought he might creep away while the men weren't looking. When he spotted a hawthorn tree close by, he climbed high into its branches and hid.

"I'm tired of digging," one man said. "You take a turn."

"Not me," said the other. "Let Pat Diver do it," and he shook that big old tree so hard that Pat came tumbling down at his feet.

Poor Pat. He took up that shovel and tossed dirt out of the grave as if his life depended on it, for it probably did. What would those huge men do if he refused? Pat dug and dug until his hands were blistered. He was exhausted and had lost all sense of time.

But the two huge men kept watching for the sunrise. Just before the first rooster crowed, they said they must go. Pat would have to finish the job himself.

"It's your lucky night, Pat Diver," one man said.

"If we could stay a little longer," said the other, "we would bury you with the corpse." And the two huge men rushed out of the graveyard.

My lucky night? Pat couldn't imagine one more ghastly. A few tears began to run down his cheeks, but he pushed the corpse into the grave and shoveled all the loose dirt back in the hole. It was all he could do to keep from sobbing. His entire body ached. He wiped off the tears with gritty fingers, staggered out of the graveyard, and trudged down the road.

For weeks afterward he shivered and shook. He couldn't mend a pot or a pan if he tried. When his hands finally stopped shaking, he resumed the tinker's trade— but wherever he roamed, he was careful to find lodging well before nightfall.

Late one afternoon, Pat found himself on a lonely mountain road. Storm clouds raced in, darkening the sky, and rain came pelting down. Pat hurried to the nearest cabin and knocked. An old man came to the door. Pat thought he looked vaguely familiar but couldn't remember where he had seen him.

"May I spend the night?" Pat asked.

"Come right in," said the old man. "Sit by the fire."

His wife called out to the barn. "Come here, boys."

Pat was horrified to see two huge men lumber across the yard and into the cabin. Their faces were almost hidden by their long, greasy hair.

"Listen," the woman told her sons. "Pat Diver has a story to tell."

Courting Astriah
GERMANY

Georg knew his future was assured now that he was apprenticed to the greatest chef in all of Germany. He was ready to look for a bride.

One day Georg was walking along the street when he noticed a long-haired maiden about fifty paces ahead. He was intrigued by the way her blood-red hair swayed from side to side as she hurried along. She must be the most beautiful maiden in the entire city of Worms, he thought to himself. He must meet her.

He followed the red-haired maiden through the twisting streets of the city until he saw her stop to unlock a door. She stepped inside so quickly that he didn't catch a glimpse of her face, but at least he had discovered where she lived. He approached her house and knocked three times, holding his breath. Would she open the door?

She didn't. But a lovely voice responded, "Who's there?"

"My name is Georg," he replied. "Soon I will be the finest chef in all of Worms, and I am looking for a lovely bride to share my good fortune."

"I would like to meet you," she answered softly, "but my parents are not well. Could you return tomorrow?"

Georg was thrilled. "Tell me your name," he said, "and I will return."

"It's Astriah," she said, and then bid him good-bye.

"What a beautiful name," replied Georg. He said good-bye and hurried home. That night he lay awake thinking about the red-haired maiden. It was close to midnight when he finally fell asleep. He dreamed that he followed Astriah through the streets of the city, just as he had done that day. But in his dream, she continued into the forest. He followed her until she reached a very old tree. He hoped she would turn around so he could see her face. But before she did, he woke up.

Georg opened his eyes, disappointed that he had not seen her beautiful face. He wanted to see how she looked. Perhaps he would that afternoon, but now he must get dressed and hurry off to work. This was his first day as an apprentice to the great chef.

. When he arrived at the inn, the chef said, "Today I will teach you how to make blood sausage." When Georg mixed the pig's blood with the other ingredients, he couldn't help but think of Astriah's beautiful red hair and how it swayed when she walked.

The chef tasted the blood sausage and told Georg he had never had an apprentice who learned so quickly. Georg was a happy man when he left the inn and set out for Astriah's house. He knocked on her door three times.

"Dear Georg," said Astriah from the other side of the wooden door. "I'm so sorry, but my parents still are not well. I can't meet you today."

Georg was both disappointed and surprised. He was disappointed that he would not meet her, but he was surprised that she knew who was knocking before he said a word. "Astriah," he said, "God willing, we will meet tomorrow."

That night Georg twisted and turned in his bed. He could not get the beautiful maiden out of his mind. At midnight, sleep finally overcame him, and he again dreamed that he followed Astriah deep into the forest. She walked past the old tree to a little hut and went inside. He crept close and peered through a crack in the door. There he saw Astriah facing a fireplace and stirring a blood-red broth. Just when he thought she might turn around, he awoke. He was even more frustrated than before, because he still had not seen her face. But it was time to go to work.

That day the chef taught Georg how to make beet soup—soup exactly the color of blood. As he stirred it, Georg couldn't help but think of the red broth that

Astriah had stirred in his dream. He took this as a sign that they were meant for each other and that she would soon be his bride. After work Georg hurried to Astriah's house.

Once again Georg knocked three times, but Astriah still did not open the door. Yet her voice seemed even lovelier than before. "My parents are too sick for me to meet you now," she said, "but at midnight I will be in front of your house, standing by the fountain in the square."

Georg was astounded. "How did you know where I live?"

"Haven't I visited you in your dreams the past two midnights?" asked Astriah.

Georg felt a chill race along his spine. She knew about his dreams even though he had not revealed them to anyone. Georg was amazed by her remarkable powers. "I will meet you there," he replied.

As midnight approached, Georg stood by the fountain, waiting anxiously. But just as the town clock struck twelve, he slumped down on the cobblestone street. His sudden need to sleep was irresistible.

Georg dreamed he was outside the cottage in the forest. He watched through the crack in the door as Astriah stirred her red broth. Her hair swayed as if it were alive each time she moved. He knocked, and Astriah invited him in. "I have been waiting for you, Georg."

He was still asleep when Astriah flew through the air

and landed beside him at the fountain. For a moment she watched him dreaming about her. Then she leaned over him, tossing her hair so that it covered his face. All at once her hair began to writhe like so many bright red serpents, each one sucking blood from his neck.

In his dream Astriah turned to look at Georg, her red hair swinging to reveal her face at last. But it was not the face of a beautiful maiden. It was the face of a wrinkled old hag, swooping down on him like a vulture and devouring him.

Georg screamed and screamed, but not a sound came forth. His heart had stopped beating. All the blood had been drained from his body.

The Shaggy Gray Arm
ICELAND

Jon's parents didn't want him to go to magic school. They had heard that some students changed in strange and mysterious ways—and some disappeared without a trace.

But Jon was determined. "How else can I chase away ghosts and demons?" he asked. "How can I overcome bullies? I must learn to write magic signs and symbols so I can protect us."

The truth was that his parents didn't want him to go to any school at all. In those days most people in Iceland believed that reading and writing were dangerous. Someone might use the knowledge for evil purposes. Even clergymen were suspect.

But, bit by bit, Jon convinced his parents that magic could be useful. Didn't they want to see the invisible little people who lived in the rocks and hillocks around their farm? The ones who slipped into the house each night to eat the food left for them on the table?

Besides, Jon promised he would be a good magician. He said he would *never* dig up a body in a graveyard and skin the lower half to make a pair of magic pants. "Who wants the coins that appear in corpse breeches?" he asked. "Not me." He said he would undo evil curses that dried up a cow's milk or left a baby crying all day. So his parents finally relented. They waved good-bye to their son with tears in their eyes. Who knew what the future held? Would they ever see him again?

Jon walked for hours. When he finally arrived at magic school, he saw smoke belching from a nearby volcano. He knocked on the school's iron door. A shaggy gray hand poked a hole through the thick iron, reached out to turn the handle, and beckoned Jon to come inside. The door groaned open. Jon looked, but he saw no one there. No shaggy gray body belonged to the shaggy gray arm. Jon did see a spiral staircase leading deep into the earth. And just as he took the first step downward, the door clanged shut behind him. Jon realized that the hole in the iron door had mysteriously closed, leaving him in inky darkness. He inched his way down, feeling for the edge of each step with his toe. Maybe the stairway seemed endless because he was moving so slowly, or maybe it really did descend to the very bowels of the earth. With each

step he grew warmer as he neared the underground caul-
drons of volcanoes.

Finally he saw a faint glow ahead. It was coming through
a doorway at the bottom of the stairs. When he entered
the cavernous room, the only light he saw was from the
fiery letters in books that students held in their hands.
No sunlight pierced the darkness of their study hall. No
teacher lectured to the class.

A boy named Magnus welcomed him, but most kept
reading. Jon knew they couldn't spare a moment from
their studies. He remembered what a storyteller had said
about the magic in the skin-covered books and how hard it
was to learn. "Seven years!" the storyteller had said. "That's
how long it takes to master everything spelled out in fiery
letters." Jon realized he would have to work hard to catch
up with the rest of the class. He had arrived weeks late,
because it took so long to convince his parents to let him
go to magic school.

Suddenly every head snapped up. It was time to eat.
The shaggy gray arm that Jon had seen at the iron door
now shoved itself through the rock wall of the classroom.
It handed each student a platter of fish along with milk in
a cup made from a ram's horn.

Jon wondered why the students were listening so in-
tently. He saw the arm withdraw and heard a muffled
shriek—just before the wall slammed shut. Who was
back there? Another student? A shaggy servant?

Some students whispered to one another. Some anxiously thumbed through their books, looking for protective spells. But others seemed to grow more menacing. After they finished eating, all quickly returned to their studies.

"How do I get a book?" Jon wondered aloud.

He didn't have to wait for long. The shaggy gray arm thrust through the cave wall and dropped the first magic book on his desk. When the arm withdrew, it left a whiff of sulfur behind. Jon snorted to get the stench out of his nose. Then he began with the easiest spells, because he was learning to read and write at the same time.

Magnus answered all of Jon's questions, much to the annoyance of some other students. They wanted to concentrate in perfect silence.

Somehow the fiery letters lit up words in Jon's mind. When he finally headed to his room, totally exhausted, the same fiery letters lit his way along the corridor as eerily as a candle.

Before he fell asleep, he saw the dim back of a student outside his door. He didn't know which one, but just as Magnus walked past, he saw the student wave his hands and mutter something.

In a puff of smoke, Magnus disappeared, and a slippery slug crept up the wall. Jon was horrified, but he sneaked into the corridor as soon as he could and put the slug safely on his closet shelf. From then on, he was wary of his classmates. Whom could he trust?

Year after year Jon studied, until he was one of the most talented magicians at the school. He finally learned how to turn the slug back into Magnus, and he shared the knowledge that Magnus had missed while making slimy trails in the closet.

Jon could cause another student's baked fish to swim right off the plate. He could turn a ram's horn cup into a wildly butting ram. He knew how to ward off ghosts and demons, and how to put special signs inside his shoes to overcome a bully. He learned demonic spells and curses, too, but he stored them in the deepest recesses of his mind, never to be used unless he was in extreme danger. After seven years, Jon and his classmates were about to return to the upper world.

All but one, that is.

A terrible rumor was being whispered about. Some student was going to disappear without a trace. Jon hadn't believed what his parents had said so long ago. But now Magnus was saying the same thing. And Magnus knew exactly how it would happen.

"We'll go up the stairs single file," he said, "and everyone will be allowed into the upper world except for the last one in line. The shaggy gray arm will grab him and carry him down to the deepest, darkest depths, where he will be a slave forever."

Jon knew he couldn't outdo that demonic gray arm with magic, but he was the leader of his class. He had to do something. So he made a plan.

"I'll leave last," Jon told his classmates. Some sneered at him for being such a fool. Magnus thanked him.

On the last day, Jon and his classmates began the long climb up the dark stairs. The shaggy gray arm was holding the iron door open at the top.

One by one his classmates exited into the first sunlight they had seen in seven years. When Jon reached the door, he saw the shaggy arm reaching for him.

"I am not the last," Jon shouted. "See the one behind me?"

Jon leaped out the door, while the shaggy arm seized Jon's shadow instead. When the arm realized what it had done, it rang that iron door like a monstrous cymbal clanging its fury all the way to the center of the earth.

Jon was free. He was almost dancing down the path.

Then he saw a demonic grin on Magnus's face. "Do you realize that whatever that gray arm takes, it never gives back?"

Jon stared at the ground where his shadow should be.

"And do you realize," Magnus asked, "what troubles you'll have with no shadow? Everyone will think you are a demon. They will run away screaming."

Jon suddenly noticed that Magnus had no shadow either.

"Welcome to my world," said Magnus, shaking Jon's hand. His grip was excruciatingly painful. Jon looked down in horror.

Creeping down Magnus's arm was a wave of shaggy gray fur.

The Prince's Fate

EGYPT

The king and queen of Egypt could hardly believe it. Was their baby boy to die some frightful death? That's what the Hathors said—the seven goddesses who could see into the future.

"Your son shall die by serpent, crocodile, or dog," they decreed. Then they left the palace without another word.

The queen wept and the king paced the floor. Would a poisonous serpent bite their son when he was a baby? Or would a crocodile from the mighty Nile River devour him when he was still a child? Or would he grow to manhood only to have a dog tear him limb from limb?

How could they protect their son?

"We must build a strong house for him, far out in the desert," said the king, "and never let him venture outside its walls." They supplied the young prince with the finest foods. He grew strong on melons, figs, dates, fish, and fowl—and special bread made with fruit and honey for the royal family.

The finest teachers taught him how to read hieroglyphics, the picture language that was inscribed on papyrus paper and in the great pyramids and tombs. He learned various board games and was given clay balls for playing catch.

Servants anointed his body with precious perfumes and oils, and they clothed him in the finest white linen. The king and queen thought their son had everything he could desire. They even sent dancers, musicians, and acrobats to entertain him.

But the prince was lonely. He climbed the stairs to the flat roof of his home and looked out across the desert. What lay beyond that vast expanse of sand?

And what was that animal he saw running and jumping and playing with the hunter passing by? The prince raced downstairs and asked one of his servants, the Inspector of Horns and Hooves and Feathers.

"That's a dog," the servant replied.

"Tell my father I must have one," said the prince.

The servant turned pale. He knew what the goddesses had decreed. "A dog?" the servant cried.

"Yes! A dog." The prince ordered the servant to race to the king's palace that very day.

The king had never said no to the prince, no matter

what his son desired. But he didn't expect him to ask for a dog. What if the very puppy he gave the prince grew up to be the dog the Hathors had warned against? "Tell my son he can't have one," he told the servant.

But the prince didn't stop asking. Every day he sent messages to his father. And each time the king visited, the boy told him, "I want a dog." The poor king didn't know what to do. Finally, he decided he must tell the prince what the goddesses had foretold.

For a moment the prince was silent. He knew full well how dangerous serpents and crocodiles could be—but a furry little dog?

"He'll be my friend," the prince told his father. "I'll raise him myself." So the king finally relented. He couldn't stand to disappoint his son. He ordered his servants to find the friendliest tail-wagging puppy in all of Egypt.

The prince named his puppy Brave One, a fine name for a royal dog. Night and day they were together, even when the prince was studying. The puppy chewed up the prince's sandals and nipped at his toes. But the prince had never been happier.

Still, he longed to see the world beyond his desert home. He grew to manhood and could no longer stand being cooped up in a house in the middle of the desert. When he saw his father, he cried out, "Let me be free. Let my fate unfold."

The king and queen feared for their son's safety, but

they knew it was time for him to find a wife, so they let him set forth into the world—his dog by his side.

"Always wear this," said the queen, and she gave her son an amulet, a piece of magical jewelry. "It might protect thee." But she turned her face aside so the prince would not see the fear in her eyes. When had the Hathors ever been wrong?

The prince rode his horse northward, followed by his loyal dog. He had been told that the chief of Nahairana had a lovely daughter, kept in a house with seventy windows, which reached seventy cubits into the sky.

The prince looked from the tip of his middle finger to his elbow—the length of a single cubit—and he tried to imagine how high seventy cubits must be. For the chief had decreed that anyone who wished to marry his daughter must scale the wall, all the way up to her topmost window. Many princes had fallen—and died.

By the time the prince reached the princess's home, his muscles were strengthened by the long journey. His hopes were high. Besides, he surely would not fall to his death. That was not a fate the Hathors had decreed. So he climbed without fear, never looking down. And when he reached the princess's window, she clasped his hand and pulled him into her room. The prince was delighted to see that she was friendly, spirited, and every bit as lovely as everyone had said.

The princess was equally pleased with the young man

and agreed to marry him, even when he told her what the Hathors had said—that a deadly serpent, or crocodile, or dog was lying in wait for him.

"Let thy dog be killed," she begged.

He would not hear of it. "Brave One is my friend." So the princess vowed to study magic spells to protect her prince.

Soon after the wedding, the princess awoke one night when Brave One growled. She wondered if she had been right about the dog after all. But as she lay quietly beside the prince, she heard a slithering sound. In the faint light of an oil lamp she could see a serpent. A poisonous cobra! It came closer and closer.

She held the dog back and began to recite an old spell, declaring that she herself was Horus, the mighty god. "Rise venom, then fall to earth. Horus spits upon thee. Thou art weak and blind. Thy head droops, for I am Horus the great magician."

Then she pulled out her dagger and chopped the serpent to bits. The prince awoke and was amazed at what she had done.

"Behold," she said. "The gods have given one of thy dooms into thy hands." The prince gave praise.

The princess not only learned spells, she acquired a magic wand made from a curved hippopotamus tusk. On its surface were carved animals, symbols, and demons that she could call upon in time of trouble.

Soon the prince and princess traveled back to Egypt,

where the prince took daily swims in the Nile. The princess and Brave One stood on the bank watching. One day a crocodile surfaced behind the prince. It opened its great jaws, ready to clamp its vicious teeth on his foot. But Brave One barked, warning him.

The prince swam quickly toward the riverbank, with the crocodile snapping its jaws behind him. The princess shook her magic wand at it. She called upon the gods for help. "Get thee back, beast of waters. Do not show thy face to Osiris. Ra shall close thy mouth. Thoth shall cut out thy tongue." The prince splashed ashore and raced up the riverbank, and the crocodile sank beneath the murky waters.

That very afternoon, the princess fashioned small crocodiles out of wax. She stabbed them with thorns, spat upon them, trampled them, and threw them in the fire to assure the death of any crocodile that lay in wait for her prince. Dozens of the menacing crocodiles sank to the bottom of the Nile that day, never to arise.

The crocodiles didn't manage to eat him, but the prince was sure that the Hathors' prophesy would come true—somehow—someday. So he embraced life while it lasted.

One morning he and Brave One hunted foxes in the desert. The prince shot an arrow but missed. Brave One chased the fox behind a huge rock lying at the base of a cliff.

The prince followed. All he saw was the dog's tail, disappearing down the foxhole. He called and called, but Brave One didn't come back, so the prince dug with his hands, throwing sand aside to make the hole bigger. He squirmed his way in and found that he was in a low passageway lined with crumbling mud bricks. Suddenly the bricks gave way beneath him, and he tumbled to the bottom of a long shaft. Very little light filtered down from the hole above. But when the prince's eyes adjusted, he could see that he was in an underground tomb with paintings and hieroglyphics on the wall.

He picked himself up from the pile of mummified cats that had broken his fall. He was merely bruised, but he was horrified to see that he had smashed some of the sacred mummies.

It was hot and humid in the tomb. A swarm of fleas began to bite him. He was brushing sand flies and gnats out of his eyes when he heard Brave One bark far above him. The dog was leaning over the edge of the hole, peering down into the gloom.

"Go home!" the prince commanded. "Go home!" He hoped that everyone would begin searching if the dog showed up without him. But Brave One was too loyal to leave his master. He tumbled down the shaft to join him.

The prince caught him but staggered backward. As he did, he stepped on a trap designed for tomb robbers—a slab of stone delicately balanced over an even deeper hole. Both the prince and Brave One went crashing through.

A vile-smelling, powdery dust swirled up around them.

And while he lay at the bottom, gasping for air, the prince saw more hieroglyphics on the wall. The faint light made it hard to see, but he slowly read aloud: "'Death shall come to him who damages this tomb.'"

He could breathe no more.

The Hathors were right. It was a dog—a brave and loyal dog—that brought about the prince's doom.

The Headless Horseman

IRELAND

Rain dripped from the brim of Morty's oil-skin hat, and sheets of lightning flashed across the sky. His coat was soaked. Suppertime was long past, but he still had miles to go. He urged his mare on, nudging her with his heels. Not that she needed much encouragement. Wasn't she the horse who jumped any fence, raced any challenger, and galloped home with the bit clamped in her teeth? She was as eager to get back to her dry stall as Morty was to reach his fireside.

"That's a girl!" he said as she galloped along the bank of the Blackwater. Morty had ridden all the way to Ballyhooley to buy a new bridle for her. Only the finest leather, stitched by the finest saddler in Ireland, was good enough for his old mare. But he had lingered too long in the village with friends. It wasn't until the sky suddenly darkened that he noticed the storm clouds roiling overhead.

His mare slowed to a trot when they reached the bottom of Kilcummer Hill. To the left were the ruins of the old church. Torrents of rain splashed off the broken walls and gravestones. Morty looked at the sky, hoping to see a break in the clouds, but all he saw was more lightning. It lit up the road. Worse yet, it lit up something unbelievable just beyond his right shoulder. His mare snorted.

Morty wiped the rain out of his eyes. There was no way that a big black horse's head could be moving along beside him—without a body and without legs. He wiped the rain out of his eyes again and blinked. But there it was, with its short ears, enormous eyes, and broad nostrils. It was higher than his mare, as if the head belonged to a much bigger horse.

Now Morty wasn't one to spook easily. If he were, he wouldn't be traveling in the dark with lightning crackling overhead. Nonetheless, he felt a bit strange riding beside a horseless head.

Just imagine how he felt when the rest of the horse appeared. Morty was dumbfounded! Another sheet of lightning had revealed a six-foot gap between the horseless head and the headless horse. Yet both parts moved steadily down the road. His mare snorted again but didn't bolt. She was every bit as hard to spook as her master.

As soon as Morty got used to the disjointed horse, he

waited for another flash of lightning. This time he finally saw a rider. The man sat high above him, partly because the black horse was so big and partly because the rider was so tall. Morty was surprised to see that he was dressed in an old-fashioned hunting coat, the kind his great-grandfather might have worn. Oddly enough, a couple of its shiny buttons were floating a full yard behind.

Every time lightning flashed, Morty looked up quickly, but he couldn't see the man's head. He finally told his mare, "He has no head at all."

"Look again, Morty," said a raspy voice that seemed to be coming from about the level of the man's waist. Lightning flashed and Morty looked. There, under the rider's right arm, was a head unlike any head Morty had ever seen. It was ashy pale, with skin pulled tight against the skull, huge black eyes, and a mouth that reached from ear to ear.

The gigantic horse's head kept moving along, followed by its body. And the hideous rider's head? It kept moving, too, back and forth, as the motion of the horse made the rider's arm move to and fro. One moment it was hidden by the rider's coat, and the next moment it was in full ghastly view.

Morty rode up the hill quietly for a spell, not wanting to do anything that might upset his strange companion. But when nothing bad happened, Morty decided to strike up a conversation. "Your honor rides mighty well."

"Humph," growled the horrible head.

Morty tried again. "That's a brave horse your honor rides."

"Humph." This time the head's answer was muffled by the man's coat.

"He looks like a fine racer."

The ghastly head swung forward, leering from ear to ear. "Will you race me, Morty?"

"Gladly—if the night weren't so dark. I don't want to lame my old mare."

"Will you take my word for your mare's safety?" asked the head, peering out from under the man's arm.

What could Morty do? He had never turned down a race or shied from a jump in his entire life. And if that headless horseman could ride a headless horse, his strange powers could surely protect an old mare.

Morty nudged her with his heels and she shot ahead. She galloped so gallantly that the horses stayed neck and neck at first. But what mortal horse could match the stride of such a monstrous competitor?

When the black horse passed the mare, the man's grisly head turned to look back at Morty, almost slipping out from under the arm that held it.

"You have a stout heart, Morty," he shouted. "I have been looking for the likes of you for a hundred years, ever since my horse and I broke our necks at the bottom of Kilcummer Hill. You're the first who dared to ride with me."

Morty urged his mare forward, and she thundered all the way to the top of the hill. When the black horse veered to the right, the mare followed. But suddenly there was nothing under her hooves. Both horses had raced off the edge of the cliff. Morty realized he and his mare were about to crash on the rocks below, but the black horse was floating through the air.

Morty cried out, "You gave your word for my mare's safety!"

"Ha!" came the ghostly reply. "You should know better than to trust a headless horseman."

The Knife
GERMANY

LONG ago, a woman died without telling her son where she had hidden his inheritance. He searched her house day and night, but he couldn't find it anywhere.

He threw open every closet and cupboard. Nothing. He dumped out every drawer. Nothing. He looked between the pages of every book. Nothing. He dug up the yard. Nothing. Finally he tore up the floors. Still nothing.

In desperation, he went to see a witch for help. She was famous throughout the land for her amazing powers. She was shrewd, too.

"Yes, yes, I'll help you," she said, "for half the inheritance."

"Well, half is better than none," the man replied. And he agreed to share whatever he found.

"Go home," she said, "so I can work my magic." The

man left, and the witch looked around until she found her very best knife. She ground its edge against a whetstone until it was sharp as a razor. Then she waited until nightfall. When she was ready for bed, she said a spell over the knife and tucked it beneath her pillow.

As soon as she fell asleep, she began to dream—and she dreamed about a demon. The demon was frantic. "Take the knife out of my heart!" he cried.

"Not until you bring me the woman who hid her son's inheritance. She must tell me where she hid it, or that knife stays exactly where it is." Then the witch woke up, and when she felt beneath her pillow, the knife was gone.

The next night, the witch went to sleep as soon as the sun set. She was eager to see if the demon would return in her dreams. He did, with the knife still in his heart. This time, the demon brought along the woman who had hidden her son's inheritance.

"Take the knife out of my heart," cried the demon. "I can't stand it."

"Not until the woman tells me where she hid her fortune."

"Why would I do that?" asked the woman. "If I had wanted my ungrateful son to know where the money was, I would have told him. Let him search for it himself."

With that the dream ended and the witch awoke. And when she put her hand under the pillow, the knife was still gone.

On the third night the witch dreamed again. By now the demon was so weak that he could barely talk. He brought his son to speak for him, and he brought the woman, too. The son said, "Please, please, take the knife out of my father's heart!"

"Not until the woman tells," said the witch. Then the demon's son dropped to his knees in front of the woman and begged her to have mercy on his father.

Finally she relented. "All right, I will reveal this much, and this much only—the money is hidden in a box." With that the dream ended.

When the witch awoke, she pronounced another spell.

She felt under her pillow, and the knife was back. It was no longer in the demon's heart.

She hurried to the man's home to tell him the clue she had wrenched from his mother's spirit. The man shouted, "What! Don't you think I searched through every box?"

"Well, look again," said the witch, "and when you find it, I want my share."

Now, as soon as she left, he tore every box apart, and much to his amazement, he found one with a false bottom. Hidden there was his mother's entire fortune.

But did the man keep his promise to share it with the witch? Not at all. He took the money and raced out of town so she wouldn't find him.

When the witch discovered he was gone, she didn't worry. That night, she cast another spell and slipped the knife under her pillow.

The Werewolf in the Forest
EASTERN EUROPE

ONE MORNING a poor man was walking in the forest when a weasel scooted across the path. The man was so startled that he jumped and yelled. The weasel was so startled that it dropped what it was carrying and raced into the underbrush. And what did the weasel drop? A ring. A shiny golden ring.

The man was dumbfounded. *Where in the world did the weasel find it?* he wondered. He picked up the ring and wiped weasel spit off on his ragged sleeve. He could see that the ring was made of gold and was covered with intricate carving. On the inside, strange letters were engraved.

The man was puzzled. He turned the ring around and around in his hand. Never had he seen anything quite so valuable or quite so mysterious. Then he remembered a tale his grandmother had told him long ago. It had to do with rings granting wishes. But what were the magic words? As he slipped the ring onto his finger, he suddenly remembered. He could almost hear his grandmother's voice saying:

"Ring of gold, ring of old, do my bidding as you're told."

He repeated her words out loud and tested them. "Bring me a bag of gold coins," he said. Out of nowhere, a small leather bag appeared and landed at his feet.

He reached for it with trembling hands. Could his wish really have come true? He tugged it open and was astonished to see gold coins inside.

He slipped the ring and the coins into his pocket, and ran out of the forest, across the fields, into the village, and to the marketplace. There he bought a new coat for himself, a new shawl for his wife, and enough food to last them for weeks.

Did this make his wife happy? Not at all. "Where did the money come from?" she demanded. All he would say was, "It's a miracle."

Well, his wife was determined to solve the mystery. She nagged him about it every day, and when he refused to tell her, she pretended to weep. "You must have stolen it," she cried. She knew very well that he was not a thief—but she also knew that he would be horrified to be called one.

"A weasel gave me a magic ring," he said.

"A likely story," she scoffed. "You expect me to believe that?"

He reluctantly led her to the chest where he had hidden the ring. The moment he opened the lid, she grabbed the ring and made a wish: "I want a huge house," she said. Nothing happened. She tried again. Still nothing happened.

"You fool," she said. "When you stole the coins, you must have stolen the ring, too."

The poor man couldn't stand having his wife think such terrible thoughts about him. So he told her the magic words.

"Is this the way you do it?" she asked. "'Ring of gold, ring of old, do my bidding as you're told.'"

"That's right," he said, never expecting that she would turn a wish against him. But she wanted that ring for herself.

She repeated the magic words and added something horrible. "Turn my husband into a werewolf and send him to the forest, where he can howl night and day."

Zap! The man vanished and a werewolf materialized in front of her. It immediately began to howl and leaped out the window, pulled into the forest by the magic wish.

The villagers were terrified when they saw the werewolf. No one dared set foot on the street after sundown.

At night they barred their doors and shivered every time they heard the anguished howling.

Meanwhile the poor man's wife was living in luxury. She now had a large house, elegant clothes, servants, jewels, and food fit for a queen. No one could imagine how she had suddenly become so rich.

Of course her husband knew. Even though he was in that werewolf's body, he could still think like a man. He hated being a werewolf and realized that nothing could help him return to his former life—except for magic. So one night, when the moon was full, he left the forest to look for the gold ring.

When he saw his wife's magnificent new home, he didn't know which room was which. He paused by each window until he heard her snoring. Now he knew that he had found her bedroom. It was all he could do to keep from howling, but he didn't want to awaken her, so he clamped his mouth shut and leaped through her window.

In the moonlight, he could see the very chest in which he had first hidden the ring. It stood by the foot of the bed, close to his sleeping wife. He took the handle in his mouth and slowly pulled the lid open. To his horror, the hinges creaked. His wife tossed and turned in her sleep, but soon she was snoring as loudly as before. He rooted around in the chest with his nose, and when he uncovered the ring, he grabbed it with his teeth and leaped out the window.

The magic words that rang through the forest that night sounded more like barks and howls, but at last the ring understood. The werewolf disappeared. *Zap!* And the poor man stood in its place.

He picked up the ring and thought hard for a moment. "'Ring of gold, ring of old, do my bidding as you're told.'" He made his wish, then tossed the ring as far as he could into a tangle of bushes.

As the man walked out of the forest, a donkey started

to bray in the distance. When he reached home, a donkey ran to meet him, braying furiously.

"I thought you would rather be a donkey than a werewolf," he said to his wife. And he entered his house, smiling.

The Secret

ITALY

For centuries, a secret had been kept high in a tower of an Italian castle. The whole family knew *something* was there. But only the grandfather knew what it was—and he wouldn't tell. Each morning he unlocked the door and entered the tower room, staying there for hours.

His granddaughter, the lady Sophia, was burning with curiosity. She figured she had as much right to know the secret as anyone else.

So one morning she tiptoed up the tower stairs behind her grandfather. She was hoping to slip into the room. But he quickly shut the door and relocked it from inside. She pressed her ear against the door. What was he doing in there?

What the lady really wanted to hear was the clink of

coins or the clatter of jewels. Her greed made her imagine all sorts of wondrous things. What if there were boxes of diamond tiaras and necklaces, just waiting for her to wear them at the next grand ball? But the only sound she heard was the occasional scratch of a fingernail. Or was it a pen on paper?

She knew, however, exactly what she smelled. Whiffs of candle smoke were seeping through cracks around the door. Why would her grandfather burn candles long before dark? She went down the stairs before the smoke made her sneeze, and hurried to the stable.

There the lady found one of the stable boys and snapped out an order. "Saddle my horse," she said, "and be quick about it." She rode into the forest looking for the hut of an old fortune-teller. It wasn't easy to find, half hidden by bushes and overgrown with vines. But the lady finally spotted it. She dismounted and threw open the door. She didn't even knock.

"What is my family's secret?" she demanded, startling the shrunken old woman.

The fortune-teller peered up at her. "Why would I look into the past? I only foretell the future."

The lady tried to contain her anger. "Then tell me my fortune!"

"Much depends . . ." the fortune-teller began. Then she paused. She was listening to an owl hooting in a tree nearby.

"A bad sign," she said. "A great disaster may await you. Let us see." She led Lady Sophia to a nearby meadow and pulled a ruby-colored goblet from her pocket. She called to a swallow—a bird of good fortune—and she called to an owl—which foretells evil. "Whichever bird alights on the rim of the goblet first will determine your success or failure."

The owl was first.

The fortune-teller shuddered. "Be careful," she said. "Do not invite trouble."

"Ha!" snorted Lady Sophia, gripping the fortune-teller's shoulder. "You'll be the one in trouble. Not me." Without so much as a thank-you, she rode back to the castle to confront her grandfather.

"Why won't you tell me?" she stormed. "I have asked you a thousand times!"

"Patience, my dear," said the old man. "You will know someday."

"Soon?" she asked.

"No. Only the oldest member of the family is permitted to know the secret. When I am gone your father will know, and when he dies, your mother will know, and when they are both gone, your older sister will know. When she dies, it will be your turn."

The lady could hardly believe what her grandfather had said. What enraged her most was that her sister would learn the secret first.

She turned on her heel and left the castle. By the time she reached the forest, she was stamping her feet. She was so angry that she almost didn't see a small spring or the scraggly herbs growing beside it. But something clicked in her mind as she went past. She looked back and saw the oval leaves and pale pink berries. They matched a drawing she had seen in a strange old book. She had read about the herbs, too.

Suddenly she knew how to learn the family secret. She pulled the herbs out by the handful, hid them under her skirt, and hurried back to the castle. When no one was looking, she grabbed a kettle of water from the kitchen and hung it over the fire in her room. As soon as the water boiled, she tossed in the herbs and watched the murky brew turn poisonous. Fury had overcome all thoughts of love and respect for her family—and greed had twisted her mind.

At breakfast, she stirred the evil mixture into her sister's porridge. At lunch, she poisoned her parents' soup. At dinner, she slipped poison into her grandfather's pudding. One by one they lay down to die. Her grandfather was last. When he was gasping for breath, he called her to his bedside. "We never harmed you, yet you killed us, thinking you would gain a treasure. But you will be sorely disappointed. Your punishment will begin when you learn what has been hidden for so long."

Lady Sophia didn't look the least bit remorseful. "What is it?" she demanded.

"It is the skull of our oldest ancestor, which must be cared for by the oldest living descendant. This is your responsibility now, and only death will free you from its power. At seven each morning, you must enter the room and close all the windows. Then light four candles in front of the skull and open the great book that lies before it. It is the history of our family. You must learn that history and add to it each day. Just think what you must write, now that you have murdered those who loved you most." His voice grew weaker. "You will find the key," he whispered, "under my pillow."

With barely a glance at her dying grandfather, Lady Sophia shoved her hand under the pillow, found the key, and raced to the tower room.

"Surely he's lying," she raged. "No one would spend each day tending a skull!"

When she unlocked the door to the tower room, she was aghast. All she saw there was a table, a chair, a large book, four candles—and the *skull*. Its hollow eyes were staring at her.

Lady Sophia wasn't afraid of old bones, so she grabbed the skull and flung it out the window. It bounced on the ground a time or two . . . and flew right back into the tower room. It grinned at her, just inches from her nose. Again she threw it as hard as she could, and again it sailed

back, still grinning. Whatever she did, it was always with her. Whether she was asleep or awake, in the castle or out, it stayed right in front of her face.

At first Lady Sophia was annoyed. She kept thrusting it away. But as time passed, she began to worry. What if it shadowed her for life? A horrifying thought. She decided it might rest if it were properly buried. So she found a shovel to dig a grave. She had to do it herself, because none of the servants would go near her with that skull hovering close by.

She went back to the forest and dug. Her back ached. She was not used to heavy labor, but she kept shoveling— and pushing that skull away. It floated right back every time, grinning its hideous grin. She threw dirt out of the hole until it was as deep as a grave. Then she stood on the edge, grabbed the skull, and flung it in.

Suddenly the hole turned into a deep pit. Flames rose from the bottom. The edge of the hole crumbled away, and Lady Sophia fell in screaming. The skull rose into the air, turning once more to grin at the lady as the dirt closed over her head and she sank out of sight. Death had freed her from its awful power.

The skull was still grinning as it flew out of the forest. Now that its relatives were dead, it was eager to haunt a new family. How about yours?

The Severed Head

PERSIA

The king of Persia was a tyrant, a terrible man who loved nothing better than chopping off heads so he could watch the blood flow.

Everyone kissed the ground before him and sang songs in his honor. How could they do otherwise?

But still the king was not happy, for his body was covered with open sores, and his head throbbed day and night. One evening he pushed aside his silver goblet and his golden plate. "What care I for food and drink," said he, "when my life is slipping away?"

His trusted vizier spoke soothingly to the king. "Somewhere there must be a physician who can cure you," he said. "I will send forth messengers to every corner of the land."

In truth, the vizier was so evil that he had no sympathy for anyone. But he knew that keeping his job—and his head—depended on how well he served his king. So the vizier sent the message far and wide. Anyone who could cure the king would be rewarded with gold and jewels, but woe to those who tried and failed.

Most physicians were reluctant to try. They knew that the king had already been given ointments, herbs, and potions of all sorts—with no success.

A few physicians came forth, hoping for vast riches. But their medicines did not help the king. So what did he do? He called for his executioner. The physicians' heads soon rolled across the palace floor.

The king was about to give up hope when he learned that a wise old physician had come to the city—someone who knew more about medical science than any other man in the world. He could identify all the plants on earth and knew their effects on the human body, good or ill.

The king summoned him to the palace, and the old man kissed the ground in front of the king's feet.

"Rise," said the king, "and tell me if you can cure me."

The physician could see the open sores on the king's hands and face, and he noticed how often the king rubbed his throbbing forehead.

"Certainly," said the physician, "and you need not drink any vile medicines or smear any ointments on your skin."

The king was amazed. "How can that be?" he asked.

"If it pleases your majesty," said the physician, "I will return to the inn to prepare a cure. Tomorrow I will bring it to the palace."

For the first time in years, the king had high hopes. So did the old physician. He had never failed before. Why would he fail now? He told the innkeeper that he was about to cure the king, but the innkeeper was horrified.

"No one can cure him," he whispered. "You must flee the city at once!"

The physician just shook his head and smiled. "Fear not," he said, "I shall be richly rewarded."

The innkeeper turned aside, muttering to himself. "How could such a wise man be so foolish?"

Back in his room, the physician took a piece of wood and fashioned it into a mallet with a hollow handle. Then he took a handful of herbs, some blades of dried grass, and a few slices of gnarled roots. He ground them into a fine powder, mixed them with a bubbling liquid, and filled the handle of the mallet with his strange concoction. Then he sealed the handle.

The next morning, the physician hurried to the palace and kissed the ground before the king.

"Rise," said the king, "and cure me."

"If it is your pleasure to ride your horse," the physician said, "I would like you to mount it now. With your right hand you can grasp the handle of this mallet. Then use it to hit the ball that is lying on the sand. Ride up to the ball and keep hitting it ahead of you until your palm gets sweaty. When it begins to tingle, you will know that the medicine has seeped out of the mallet and into your hand. Then you must bathe and go to bed."

The king did exactly what the physician asked, and when he awoke the next day he was overjoyed. He was cured. His skin was clear and his head no longer throbbed. He sent for the physician, poured gold coins into his hands, and insisted that he sit in a place of honor beside the royal throne.

Now this was the very place where the vizier had always sat giving advice to the king. As the days went by, the physician continued to sit there, entertaining the king with stories of his travels.

The vizier became more and more jealous. When the physician returned to the inn one evening, the vizier asked the king's permission to speak.

"Your majesty," he said, "you are in grave danger. If the physician can cure you by putting something in your hand, he can kill you just as easily. I think he is a spy from another kingdom. When he has gained your trust, he will kill you."

"How can you be so suspicious?" shouted the king. "Wasn't he the only man in the world who could cure me?"

"I am thinking only of your safety," the vizier replied.

At first the King ignored the vizier. But each day, he

worried more. He watched the physician for signs of betrayal. He saw none. Yet his fears grew.

One morning, after the physician sang a song in the king's honor, the king suddenly turned cold and cruel. He beckoned to his executioner and pointed to the old physician. "Off with his head," he ordered.

The physician grew pale. "Is this the way you reward me for curing you?"

"If you could cure me by putting something in my hand, then you have the power to kill me," the king said.

"Spare me, and Allah will spare you," cried the physician. "Kill me and Allah will kill you."

But the king would not listen.

The physician continued to beg for mercy, but finally he realized there was no hope. His legs felt weak and his hands were trembling, but he asked for two last favors.

"Will you grant me a day to arrange for my burial and to distribute my books of medicine?" asked the physician. "And will you grant the favor of keeping my most precious book in your royal library?"

"Only because you cured me," said the king, and he sent the physician back to the inn, guarded by four strong men.

The next morning, the physician appeared at the palace looking old and weary, but he had accepted his fate. After kissing the ground before the king, he showed him the precious book.

"Why should I treasure it?" asked the king.

"It has special powers," said the physician. "If you want my head to speak to you after you cut it off, turn three pages of this book and read the three lines you see there. Then I will be able to answer any question you ask."

The king was astounded. He had never seen a severed head speak. He eagerly reached for the book.

"But first, my head must be pressed down on this tray on which I have sprinkled a special powder. It will stop the bleeding."

The king didn't hesitate for a moment. He ordered the execution to begin. A kindly king might have turned away from such a horrible sight. But not this king. He could hardly wait to see a speaking head.

After the executioner had performed his grisly task, he pressed the physician's head on the powdered tray.

Suddenly the physician's eyes lit up—and the head spoke. "It's time to open the book."

The king tried to turn the pages, but they were stuck together, so he licked his finger and tried again. Now he could turn the pages, but he found nothing written there.

"Turn some more," said the head. The king licked his finger again, turning page after page. Still he could find no writing. He began to feel ill, so he asked his vizier to continue.

The vizier began to turn the pages. But so many were stuck, he had to lick his finger again and again. He, too,

began to feel ill. He stopped and looked at his hand in horror. It was purple. He looked up and saw that the king was also turning purple, all the way up to his eyebrows.

"This book is poisoned!" the vizier cried. But it was too late. Both the king and the vizier tumbled to the floor—dead.

The physician's head smiled. "Just punishment for tyrants," it said, and the light went out of its eyes forever.

The Dangerous Dead
CHINA

Four travelers planned to spend the night in a roadside inn, but they arrived too late. The inn was full, and there was nowhere else to stay.

The innkeeper looked them over. He could see that they were not dressed in the manner of that region. Obviously they had come from afar. Who would know if something happened to them? Who would care?

The innkeeper tugged at his ear, pretending to think things over. "Maybe I can help you after all," he said, "if you don't mind sleeping in a room with a corpse."

The startled men looked at one another. But the night was damp and cold. They didn't want to freeze, so they accepted the innkeeper's offer.

"Wait here while I prepare things for you," he said, and a few minutes later he led them down the path to the women's quarters. He placed a small oil lamp on the table. Its light was dim, but the men could see a coffin at the end of the room. "My daughter-in-law died today," he said. "But you might as well use the sleeping couches here."

The men were exhausted. They had been walking for days. They ignored the unpleasant smell that hung in the room, flopped down, and began to snore—except for one. He was feeling uneasy about sharing a room with a corpse.

He lay awake, staring at the ceiling. He was still awake when the inn grew quiet. The stillness of midnight had descended. But now he heard a new sound, a faint rustling—something was moving at the far end of the room. He was appalled to see that it was the corpse . . . rising up in the coffin.

The next thing he knew, she climbed out and slipped quietly over to the table. He closed his eyes down to slits, pretending to sleep. But he watched as she pulled forth a strange stick of incense and lit it with the lamp's flame. As soon as dark smoke began curling up, she turned her head away, keeping the incense at arm's length.

She crept up to the sleeping men and held the incense close to the nose of one snoring traveler. As he inhaled the poisonous vapors, his snoring lessened, then ceased. She proceeded to the second man. Then the third.

I'm next, thought the fourth traveler. But when she brought the stick of incense up to his nose, he held his breath. After she turned away, he managed to breathe so shallowly that she did not hear him.

When she climbed back into the coffin, he quietly stretched out one foot and kicked the traveler nearest him. There was no response. He kicked again. Still no response.

But the corpse heard him. She rose out of the coffin and picked up the smoking incense. Again she held it up to his nose, but longer this time. When she finally moved away, he was about to explode. But he forced himself to breathe faintly.

The corpse must have thought she had killed all four travelers, because she began robbing them. She shoved the first one's body this way and that until she had found all the coins he was carrying, then she moved on to the next.

The fourth traveler knew it wouldn't be long before she came to rob him. He waited until she took her first handful of coins back to the coffin. Then he quietly slid his legs over the edge of the couch.

Before she turned around, he leaped up. But the corpse was at his heels by the time he raced out the door. He ran shrieking up the path to the inn . . . and right on past. He was afraid he couldn't awaken anyone in time to help. So down the road he went, faster than he had ever run in his entire life. He headed for the town, hoping to find safety there. At first he put some distance between himself and the corpse, but then he began to run out of breath. The corpse started to gain on him.

Just when he thought his legs were going to give out, he saw a monastery and pounded on the door. When no one opened it, he hid behind a tree.

That's when the corpse caught up with him. She darted to the right of the tree, and he dodged to the left. She darted to the left, and he dodged to the right. As they danced around, the tree creaked, bending slightly from side to side. Was it trying to block her?

So it went—the traveler scared, the corpse furious—right to left, left to right until they were exhausted. They stood panting, one on each side of the tree. Then she made her move.

She held half of the poisonous incense in each hand and thrust herself directly at the tree. With one arm on each side, she thought she would surely catch him which-ever way he went. But at that moment, a tree root tripped the traveler. He fell backward, out of her reach.

The corpse tried to pull away from the tree, but she couldn't. Her arms were stuck, entangled in the tree's bark. And on the ground, the incense lay smoldering.

The traveler arose, dazed. He saw that the corpse was no longer moving, but he wasn't sure why. Had the in-cense poisoned her? Or had the tree caught her? The trav-eler circled the tree, keeping his distance from the corpse. Then he started down the road. He knew he couldn't do anything for his three friends. They were dead. But he could tell the innkeeper about his daughter-in-law.

When the traveler appeared at the inn door, he was disheveled and trembling. The innkeeper seemed frightened to see him. Why hadn't this man suffered the fate of his three companions?

The traveler leaned against the door frame, exhausted. "Your daughter-in-law's body is stuck to a tree."

"What do you mean?" the innkeeper cried. Had something gone wrong? Had he lost his partner in crime? "I want to see for myself," he said. "Take me to her."

The traveler sank down on the doorstep. What if the corpse rose up again? He shuddered so violently that his voice quivered. "You go," he said.

The innkeeper kept asking, but the traveler refused to lead him to that terrible corpse.

"Then I must find her myself," said the innkeeper. "Tell me the way."

When the innkeeper reached the tree, he didn't see his daughter-in-law. He thought he had found the wrong tree—until he saw the edge of her robe and some long, black hairs sticking out of the bark. He watched in horror as they, too, disappeared, pulled into the tree. Now he knew. The tree had swallowed his daughter-in-law whole.

The Haunted Bell
SPAIN

Everyone in the Spanish village was frightened by the bell hanging in the marketplace. It was rusty and cracked and sounded so terrible that its bell rope was allowed to rot away. But that didn't stop it from ringing. It spooked the villagers by ringing itself. Even worse, its odious clanking meant trouble. Murders, floods, plagues, wars. Every time that bell rang, it brought forth disaster.

No one dared to take it down. One man had tried. But the moment his hands touched the bell, they stuck to the metal. Sparks flew. He writhed in agony until he finally managed to break free.

The bell had hung in the marketplace for as long as anyone could remember, but few knew its history. Those who did whispered the story behind closed doors.

It all began when a cruel baron lived in a castle high on a cliff above the village. He ordered his blacksmith to make a special suit of armor. But he knew that the blacksmith hated him—and so did everyone else.

The baron was very suspicious. He didn't know if he could trust the blacksmith to fashion armor strong enough to withstand a sword's blow. Nor did he trust him to make it so that rust could never take away its protective power.

When the blacksmith carried the armor into the great room of the castle, the baron inspected each piece. He put on the helmet and closed its visor, peering out through the holes. Then he pulled it off and thumped the chest plate with his fist. He felt the thickness of the metal plates that would cover his feet, and he saw how smoothly the metal gauntlets would flex when his hands were inside. He fingered the black plume atop the helmet and decided the armor would do. Then he dismissed the blacksmith with a wave of his hand.

The blacksmith hurried from the castle, happy to escape with his life. He knew the baron would have pulled forth his sword and murdered him if there had been so much as a scratch or a dent in the shiny metal.

The baron loved his new armor. He might have thought otherwise if he could have foreseen the future. But he was imagining how ferociously he could fight, protected by the sturdy metal. He could hardly wait to get into bloody battles, but first he had to gather everything he needed for going to war.

That very night, he left his castle on horseback, riding down the steep road to the peasants' huts. He pounded on their doors. "Give me all your money," he thundered, "and I will free you from future rents." Now the peasants knew the baron never kept his promises, but most were too frightened to resist. If they argued, they lost their lives.

When the baron rode off to battle the next spring, he was wearing his shining armor. The peasants watched until he disappeared around a curve in the road. Then they hugged one another. Some cried with relief. Others danced in the fields.

The peasants felt as if a black cloud had been lifted. They dared step outside their huts at night. No men were found hanging from tree limbs the next morning. No maidens or small children disappeared into the castle, never to be seen again.

Years passed. The walls of the baron's mighty fortress were not maintained. Water leaked through holes in the roof. Some of the heavy beams began to rot. But the peasants were happy—until one terrible day when the baron came riding home.

It was obvious that his temper had not improved while he was away, nor had his fortune. He whipped the peasants for neglecting his castle and demanded that they pay rent for the time he was gone. If they could not pay him, he set fire to their huts—usually at night. That's when he liked to ride about the countryside, spreading terror wherever he went. The peasants appealed to the king, but the baron ignored the royal decrees and killed the royal messengers.

When the peasants began to revolt, the baron just laughed. But his night rides turned sour. There seemed to be a peasant hiding behind every tree, hurling rocks at him before melting away in the darkness. The baron decided to wear his armor day and night. Finally he shut himself up in his stronghold and stationed guards at the entrance. But still he underestimated the peasants' anger.

One moonless night, a band of peasants managed to scale the treacherous cliff at the back of the castle. It was unguarded, because the baron believed that no one could approach from that side. The peasants crept toward the front, waiting in the shadows until the guards fell asleep. Then they overcame the guards, set fire to the drawbridge, and threw burning torches into the castle. It was a terrifying sight. Flames leaped high, turning the great stronghold into smoldering ruins.

Many of the servants managed to flee, but the baron was not among them. The peasants were uneasy. They wondered if the baron could have escaped the flames. If he had, he would be eager to kill them.

No one went near the castle for days, but when the embers cooled, a few brave men made their way into the ruins. There they found the baron. But not where they expected him. He was hanging from a charred beam in the great hall—dead. He was wearing his armor, with the visor closed.

The peasants were stunned. Did the baron's servants find him overcome by smoke on the night of the fire? Did they hang him to make sure he never whipped them again?

The news spread quickly. But none thought the baron deserved a decent burial. So he was left there for months, swinging in the wind until one wild night, a bolt of lightning flashed through the armor and knocked him to the floor.

When the storm moved past, peasants were startled to see an eerie light moving through the ruined castle. It continued out to the ruined stable, rising to the height of a man on horseback. Then it came bobbing down the hill, closer and closer. The peasants rushed into their huts and bolted the doors. When they heard hoofbeats and the clank of spurs, they dove into their straw beds. But nothing could protect them from the ghostly horse and rider. Once again, terror filled their nights. Huts were burned. Men, women, and children disappeared. The baron was far more cruel dead than alive.

The frightened peasants went deep into the forest to ask an old hermit for advice. He told them they needed garlic. "Chew it. Mix it with spittle. Add salt if you have it." The peasants were confused.

"Climb into trees that lean over the road—and when the baron rides by, spit on his armor. Not once, not twice, but three times. Mark my words." The peasants were even more confused. "You'll see," said the hermit.

Entire families hid in trees at night, spitting down on the baron. He didn't seem to notice. But as the peasants watched, the eerie light surrounding the armor began to fade. The shining metal started to rust. In a matter of weeks, the glow was gone.

Then one night the baron slid out of his saddle and

tumbled to the ground. His ghostly horse disappeared in the mist. Before he could struggle to his feet, peasants dropped from the trees and threw chains around him. The next morning they hauled him to court. Imagine how fearful they must have been!

The judge was trembling when he asked the prisoner his name. There was no response. The judge asked again. The baron didn't answer. The judge began to get annoyed when the baron refused to speak a third time. He said, "Open your visor." Still the prisoner stood defiantly before him.

Finally a brave peasant rushed over. He pried open the baron's visor and screamed in horror.

There, inside the rusty helmet, was . . . nothing . . . absolutely nothing. Yet still that empty suit of armor was flexing its fingers and moving its feet.

The judge choked out his verdict. "I order you to be hanged at dawn." But the peasants objected.

"That didn't kill him before," one cried. "Take him to the blacksmith's forge. Turn him into . . ." and here he faltered.

"A bell," said the judge. "If he's a bell, he can do no harm."

But it was almost as if the blacksmith had been sentenced as well. When he hammered the armor, it groaned and writhed. When he thrust it into the smelting furnace, it shrieked and reached out to grab the blacksmith with fingers of hot metal. Lightning streaked out of the furnace, and thunder almost deafened him.

The blacksmith thought he was losing the battle, until suddenly he remembered the hermit's advice. He grabbed a clove of garlic, tossed it into his mouth, and chewed on it. Then he spat at the molten metal, once, twice, thrice. His spit sizzled and turned into steam. But he finally subdued the armor and made it into a bell.

The bell was hung in the marketplace, so the peasants could see that the dreaded armor would no longer stalk them at night.

But the very first time the bell was rung, it cracked and spit out a shower of sparks. The peasants backed away, whispering to one another. Was the ghost trying to slip out the crack? Or would it haunt the bell forever? No one knows . . . except for the baron.

The Gruesome Test

JAPAN

Suitors came from all over Japan to woo a beautiful maiden. First they fell in love with her— then they ran away. Some were heard screaming as they raced down the road.

Suspicious neighbors spread rumors. They suspected that the maiden might actually be a goblin or a fox-woman. Her parents were mystified. Why did their lovely daughter terrify young men? She was gentle, happy, and hardworking. She didn't complain when helping her mother around the house and never wasted a single grain of rice when she cooked their meals.

What more could parents desire? Grandchildren. That's why the couple wanted their daughter to marry. Besides, the aging father needed a strong son-in-law to help him grow rice—and he needed him soon.

Arranged marriages had been the tradition for as many generations as anyone could remember. But long ago the father had decided to let his beloved daughter choose a husband for herself. One spring he began to regret his decision. He sat beneath a flowering cherry tree, watching pink petals fall to the ground. Would his daughter's youth fade away as quickly as the delicate flowers? Just as he was losing hope that she would ever marry, a soldier came striding up to the house.

"May I court your daughter?" asked the bold young man.

The father liked his broad shoulders and muscular arms, good for planting rice. "Come right in," he said, and he happily introduced the young man to his daughter.

The maiden moved gracefully about the room, serving the soldier tea and rice. She seemed shy, speaking softly and lowering her eyes. The young man seemed smitten. When the meal was over, she accompanied him to the door and quietly invited him to come back.

"But not until midnight," she whispered, "and knock lightly so you do not awaken my parents."

He was surprised, but not half as surprised as he was when he returned that night. The moment he entered the house, she made a very strange request.

"You must promise on your honor," she whispered, "that you will submit to a test of your love for me. And promise that you will never tell a living soul what that test is."

The young man couldn't imagine what the maiden had in mind—but he agreed to remain silent. "On my honor, I will never tell."

"Then wait here," she said. She slid open the paper screen to her room and closed it behind her. The soldier waited impatiently. When she returned, she was wearing a loose white garment. Oddly enough, the handle of a shovel poked out from under the hem.

"Follow me," she whispered. They moved through the village under a cloudy sky, with only fleeting glimpses of the moon. On such a night, ghosts were said to wander. The soldier followed the white figure ahead of him, careful not to awaken sleeping dogs. They slipped through the village streets to the woods beyond, hurrying down the dark road until they reached an ancient cemetery.

When the moon emerged from the clouds, they could see old gravestones covered with moss and mold. Here and there, bamboo cups held wilted flowers. Weathered statues of gods stood guard, protecting souls.

The maiden stopped by a grave that looked quite fresh. She pulled forth her shovel and began to dig, flinging clods of dirt to one side. Then she dropped to her knees and swept aside dirt with her hands. The soldier could see that she had uncovered a small coffin.

Imagine his surprise when she lifted the lid, opened the white shroud, and tore an arm off the corpse inside. Then she clamped it in her teeth and took a large bite.

"If you love me, you will eat what I eat," she cried, ripping the other arm off the corpse and tossing it to the soldier.

He didn't hesitate. He took a large bite himself. Now he was even more surprised. He was eating a candy corpse, made of sugar and rice flour.

The maiden burst out laughing. "You are the only one of my suitors who did not run away. I want to marry a brave husband, and you are the one."

You would think that the soldier would laugh, too. The maiden was not a monster, after all. But he glowered at her. "Only candy!" he said. "I thought you were giving me much more." He grabbed her shovel and began to dig up a real grave.

This time it was the maiden who ran away screaming.

The Enchanted Cave

SPAIN

Peregil didn't need the moonlight to find his way to the ancient well. The water carrier and his faithful donkey had trudged up the steep path thousands of times to fill their earthenware jugs with water. Usually they didn't work this late, but the night was hot, and thirsty townsfolk were still in the streets. "Perhaps I can sell another jugful," Peregil told his long-eared companion.

They entered the abandoned fortress that rose high above Granada and proceeded to the well. The great battlements of the Alhambra—with its watchtowers, fountains, and elaborately decorated rooms—had been built centuries earlier when Moors ruled that part of Spain. The wells they had dug were as impressive as their fortress, because the shafts reached all the way down to the purest, coolest water.

Peregil was about to fill his large jugs when he heard a feeble cry. A gnarled hand beckoned to him from a stone bench just beyond the well. The water carrier hurried over to find out what was wrong. In the moonlight he could see an old man lying there, dressed in Moorish garb. His voice was faint and raspy.

"I will give you twice what you could earn for your jugs of water," he said, "if you will let your donkey carry me to the city instead."

"God forbid," cried Peregil, "that I should charge a man in such trouble." He hoisted the Moor onto his donkey and steadied him as they moved down the path, keeping him from falling onto the rough ground. They descended so slowly that the streets were empty by the time they reached the city.

Peregil asked the man where he was going. "Alas," he said, "I don't know anyone here. But if you will let me spend the night at your home, you will be rewarded."

The water carrier knew that the very lives of Moors and Jews were endangered, because the Inquisition was raging in Spain. Peregil had already been harassed by government officials for merely *befriending* non-Christians like the Moor. But how could he abandon someone in need? He nodded to the old man, and led his donkey home along the shadowy back streets. His biggest worry was what his wife would say when he helped the Moor into their house.

"You will bring trouble down on our heads," she cried the moment she saw him.

"He's sick," Peregil said. "We can't leave him in the street." He placed a mat and a sheepskin on the floor and helped the old man lie down. Peregil and his wife continued to argue while the Moor slept. But when the man began to shake uncontrollably, Peregil rushed to his side.

"My life is about to end," the old man whispered, "but I want to reward you for your kindness." He slipped a shaking hand beneath his robe and pulled forth a small sandalwood box. "This is for you." Then he mumbled only a word or two more before he drew his last breath.

Peregil thought that he might have said "treasure," but he wasn't sure. Besides, he was much too upset about the man's death to even think about what the box might contain.

His wife broke into tears. "Now we will be accused of murder!"

"Just help me!" Peregil replied. The two of them managed to roll the sleeping mat around the corpse and heave the bundle onto the back of the donkey.

It was still dark out, so Peregil led his donkey to the riverbank and buried the corpse in the sand. Then he led the donkey back home and went to sleep. He was sure that no one had seen him bring the Moor into his house or take his body away.

Unfortunately, a gossipy neighbor had been peering

out the window that night. He was the local barber, and he loved gathering scraps of news to pass along to his customers. He had watched Peregil arrive with the Moor, and he had seen him take the body away. The barber had even thrown on his clothes and shadowed the water carrier all the way to the river, where he saw him bury the corpse.

The next morning, the barber rushed to the house of his first customer, a corrupt government official. He was early, but he could hardly wait to share his news.

"Last night I saw robbery, murder, and a burial," he gasped, still out of breath from running. He dramatized every detail that he could remember or could imagine.

The official's eyes opened wide. There was opportunity here. If there had been a robbery, there must be a pile of money that the scheming official could claim for himself—supposedly in the name of justice.

The barber had barely begun the haircut when the official shoved him aside and stormed out of the house to find Peregil.

The water carrier had arisen early to fill his jugs. He was already walking through the city, shouting, "Who wants water from the well of the Alhambra, cold as ice and clear as crystal?"

"I want more than water," barked the official, grabbing Peregil by the collar. "Tell me where you have hidden the booty."

Peregil turned pale. "I robbed no one," he cried.

The official shook him. "I know everything," he said. "I could throw you in jail for murder." His eyes narrowed. "But it was only a Moor. Maybe I can look the other way if you give me the Moor's money."

Only a Moor? Peregil couldn't understand such cruelty. "God smite me if I lie. I did not kill the Moor, but he did leave me a sandalwood box."

He was so sure that the official would not be interested in what was inside the box that he took him home to see it. The official grabbed the box, but he was terribly disappointed when only a scroll with Arabic characters and the stub of a wax candle tumbled out.

The greedy official lost interest in Peregil's case. Obviously there was no money to be had. He listened briefly to the water carrier's explanations and decided he was innocent. He allowed Peregil to keep the useless box—but not his donkey. That he kept for himself. "In payment of costs and charges," he said, even though no payment was due, and he led the donkey away.

Poor Peregil. Not only had he lost his beloved, four-footed companion, he would have to carry the heavy water jugs on his own back.

When he told his wife, she was furious. "I warned you!" she cried. "You never should have brought the Moor into our home. And all you got was a worthless sandalwood box!"

Peregil took her scolding for only so long. Then he

snatched the box from a shelf and threw it on the floor.
The parchment scroll fell out. When it unrolled, the water
carrier noticed how much writing was on it, and he began
to wonder what it said.

That very day he took it to a friend, a Moorish shopkeeper. "Can you read this to me?" he asked.

The shopkeeper studied it for a moment. Then his eyes
brightened. "This is a spell," he said, "to break open the
door to an enchanted treasure lying beneath the Alhambra's highest watchtower. It says that even the strongest
bolts and bars—even rock itself—will yield to the words
written here."

Peregil was mystified. Could this possibly be true? He
watched anxiously as the Moor continued to read the Arabic characters. "Unfortunately it is worthless," his friend
said, "unless a certain candle, made with precious per-
fume, is burned at the same midnight hour that the magic
spell is spoken."

"I think I have a stub of such a candle," cried Peregil.
"It was in the same sandalwood box." He rushed home to
retrieve it, then carried it back to his friend's shop.

"This is the very candle," the Moor said, "that is speci-
fied in the scroll. While it burns, the secret cave will remain
open. But beware! He who stays near the treasure after the
candle is extinguished will be trapped there, enchanted
forever. Perhaps you need me to go along."

The generous water carrier was quick to respond. "Of

course," he said, "I need you to invoke the spell, and we will share any treasure it reveals." That very night, Peregil and his friend climbed the steep path to the Alhambra, veering to one side to reach the base of the watchtower. They clambered through brush and over rocks until they found the enchanted place described in the scroll. Both men carried lanterns to light up the underground passages. But first they had to tear away the vines and shrubs that hid the entrance to the cave.

Once inside they found steps carved into stone. They descended from one chamber to another . . . and another . . . and another. It grew damper and darker and drearier the farther down they went. The cave smelled of wet earth and rock. Water from the ceiling dripped on their heads. Both men had to quell a desire to flee—to race out of that strange and forbidding place. But when they stepped onto the floor of the fourth chamber, they knew that the treasure they were seeking was trapped somewhere beneath their feet.

When the clock struck twelve in the watchtower above them, they could hear it faintly in the cave. They lit the candle stub and breathed in its strong scent of myrrh. But there wasn't a moment to lose. The shopkeeper quickly read the magic spell aloud before midnight passed.

There was a horrendous rumble beneath them. The stone floor on which they were standing shook and gaped open, revealing yet another flight of steps. The men felt even more inclined to flee, but they begged mercy from whatever powers they had unleashed, took strength from each other, and descended into the final chamber.

If they had been frightened before, they were terrified now. For their lanterns let them see who was guarding the treasure. On each side stood a huge Moor, dressed for battle, with sword drawn. Peregil backed away, pulling his friend with him. But suddenly he stopped.

"Look!" Peregil whispered. "They aren't blinking an eye."

The shopkeeper laughed hysterically. A moment before, he had thought he would die, and now he realized he could be the richest man in all of Granada.

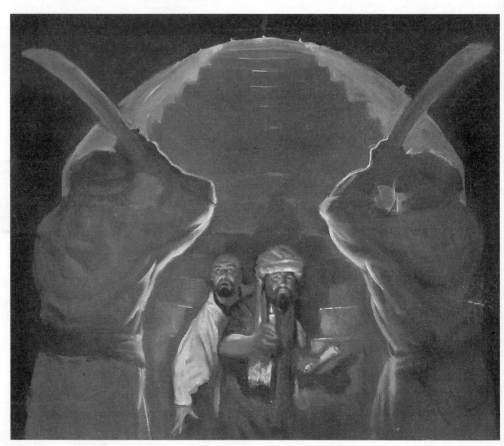

"Of course," he said, when he finally caught his breath. "It was written on the scroll. If someone is in the treasure chamber when it closes, he is enchanted forever."

Peregil began to load a bag with gold and silver and jewels from elegant porcelain jars. His friend grabbed treasure by the fistful. But both men kept a wary eye on the two guards, still standing like statues on each side of a huge banded chest. Peregil wondered what was inside it.

He inched past the nearest guard so he could open the lid. But the moment he touched it, there was a noise in the chamber above. Was it a falling rock? Or were the stairs about to be blocked by mysterious powers? The frightened men raced up the steps and stumbled into the upper chamber. That's when the candle stub slipped from Peregil's hand and fell to the floor. Its flame went out. Immediately the earth began to rumble and the stone floor slammed shut beneath them. The steps that led down to the treasure were now hidden under a thick layer of rock.

Peregil grabbed the candle stub, and the men ran up to the entrance of the cave. They were happy to be safe, with their bags filled with treasure. On the way down the rocky path, they chattered about what they could do with their newfound wealth. But before they reached the city, the shopkeeper took hold of the water carrier's shoulder.

"You know what will happen," he said, "if the officials ever hear of our treasure. They will take our money and throw us in jail besides. So we must not tell anyone." But as luck would have it, a bright jewel slipped from Peregil's bag and fell beside his doorstep. It gleamed in the moonlight. He didn't notice it, but his nosy neighbor did. That nasty gossip watched until Peregil disappeared into the house. Then he sneaked over and pocketed the jewel. The moment the sun rose, he showed it to the corrupt official.

The official was outraged. He raced down the street and burst through Peregil's door. "I'll throw you in jail yet," he shouted, slapping the poor water carrier, "unless you give me the money you stole."

What could Peregil do? He would rather lose his treasure than his freedom, so he told the official about the enchanted cave.

Was the official satisfied with Peregil's coins and jewels? "I want more," he demanded. "Take me to the cave tonight."

Peregil didn't want to involve the storekeeper. But if the Moor did not read the scroll, the treasure room would not open, the official would be furious, and Peregil would rot in jail.

"I'll bring someone to help us," Peregil said. He hoisted the bag of treasure onto his shoulder and took it to the official's home. Then he raced off to find the Moor to beg for his assistance.

"What will become of us?" cried the shopkeeper. But as much as he feared the official's power, he could not desert his friend.

That night, Peregil and the shopkeeper waited by the steep path until the official joined them. He showed up riding Peregil's donkey. It brayed when it saw its old master, and Peregil stroked its long ears. "Let's be off!" snapped the official, and when the donkey was slow to move, he poked and prodded it. That greedy man considered it nothing more than a beast of burden.

They climbed the steep hillside to the cave, with the official muttering all the way about the rough ride. Then Peregil tied his old donkey to a tree, and all three men descended to the chamber directly above the treasure. Peregil lit the candle at midnight, and the shopkeeper read the magic words spelled out on the scroll.

When the official heard the horrendous rumble and saw the floor open over another set of descending steps, he was terrified by the powers invoked. "I'll stay here," he said. "You bring the treasure up to me." But he was not satisfied with the bags of money and jewels the two men brought up from the huge jars.

"Is this all?" he asked.

"We'll break the poor donkey's back," cried Peregil, "if we make it carry more. I won't bring up another coin."

"Nor I," said the shopkeeper.

Only greed could overcome the official's fear. "Then I will get more for myself," he said. But he had barely started down the steps when he turned back. "Give me the candle and scroll," he demanded, grabbing them from the two men. He wanted to be sure that no fearsome powers were invoked while he was in the chamber below. Then he descended, with candle and lantern lighting his way. His knees almost buckled when he saw the enchanted Moorish guards, but when he spotted the magnificent treasure chest, he was thrilled. What incredible wealth must lie inside!

He set the candle down beside the lantern and struggled to open the chest's heavy lid. It was stuck. He pushed and pried and pushed again—and all the while the candle stub was burning lower. He didn't notice when it flickered out.

A horrendous rumble vibrated throughout the cave. The water carrier and the shopkeeper had been peering down the steps, but they jumped back the moment they felt the stones shaking. The floor beneath their feet crashed shut. The men were stunned. The prediction on the scroll had come true.

The greedy official was trapped—enchanted forever.

It took a moment for the two friends to realize their good fortune. They were *free*! They picked up the bags of treasure and hurried up the steps. No one saw them emerge from the cave. Not even the gossipy neighbor. He had gone to bed early, too tired that night to cause any trouble.

But the donkey was there—the beloved donkey that the official had stolen. Peregil hugged its furry neck. "I can take you home!" The men headed down the path, thankful that they had escaped with their lives. Never again could that greedy official mistreat man or beast. And never again would anyone plunder the treasure beneath the Alhambra—for the scroll and candle were buried forever.

The Witch of the Woods

EASTERN EUROPE

Princess Sybil loved to explore the vast forest that lay at the edge of her parents' kingdom. She didn't worry about creatures lurking there. What harm could befall her?

"If you're not careful," warned the queen, "the Witch of the Woods will catch you."

Sybil smiled at her mother. But nothing could stop her from walking in the forest. She didn't even believe in witches. So she continued to slip out of the castle whenever she could. One day she heard an owl hooting deep in the woods. She followed the sound until she saw the bird perched in an old pine tree. She wanted a closer look, but when she began to climb up the tree, the owl disappeared around the other side.

Sybil kept climbing and grabbed a branch that felt squishy on the outside and hard within.

It grabbed back! It wasn't a branch at all. It was a sinewy and gnarled old arm.

"Gotcha!" said the Witch of the Woods.

The next thing the princess knew, she was nose to nose with the most hideous creature she had ever met. The witch leaned around the tree trunk to get a good look at the princess. The princess leaned away as far as she could. But the witch held tight. Sybil had never seen anyone quite so awful. The witch's hair was a tangle of dead weeds. Her face was as wrinkled as a dried apple. The skin on her arms looked like crumpled tree bark. And her eyes! Those horrible, glowing eyes! The princess was afraid they would burn right through her. Why, oh, why had she doubted her mother's warning?

"I've been hoping to catch a lovely young girl," rasped the witch. "I won't let you go unless you promise to give me your first love. I want a young husband."

The princess had no idea who her first love would be. But the thought of giving anyone to the witch was appalling. Sybil forced herself to stare right into the witch's glowing eyes.

"I won't do it," she said.

"Oh yes, you will," cackled the witch. "Or I will make you my slave."

The princess was scared, but she wasn't going to let the witch know. "If you do," she said, "my father and his warriors will kill you."

The witch hooted. "How could anyone kill me? No one can find me."

"I just did," said the princess.

"Oh no, you didn't," said the witch. "*I* found *you*. But I'll make you a bargain. If you can find where I live within three days, I'll claim neither you nor your first love."

"And if I don't?"

The witch clutched the princess's arm so hard that her long fingernails dug in. "If you *don't* . . . I will marry your first love, *and* I'll make you my slave besides."

The princess knew it was a wretched bargain. Just three days? To find a witch who could supposedly change herself into any animal or bird on earth, or hide under a rock if she pleased?

"I won't agree unless you give me a clue," said the princess, trying to keep her teeth from chattering.

The witch thought for a moment. "Clues won't help you," she said, "but here's one:

"Where the scorpion's voice resounds,
Find one who is and is not bound."

She let go of the girl's arm, turned herself into an owl, and flew away.

The princess lowered herself from limb to limb until she reached the ground. She slowly walked back to the castle. What was she going to do? Did she dare ask the king or queen for help? If she did, they would know she'd

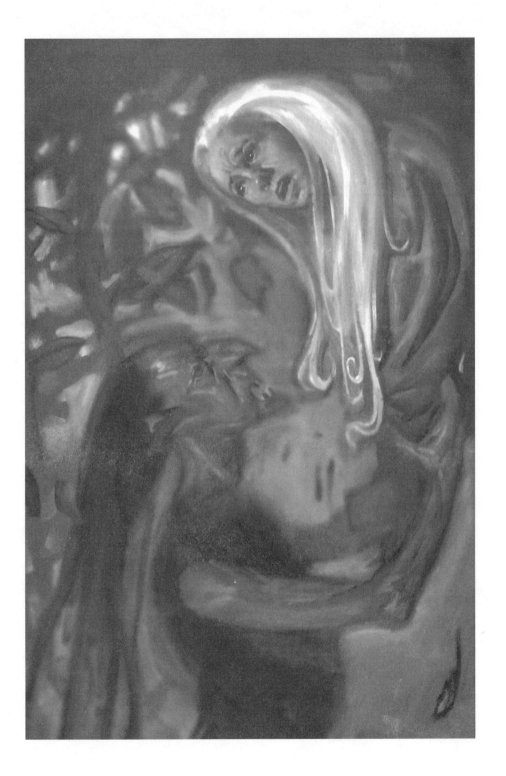

been in the forbidden forest. She was still trying to decide when she entered the castle, but her parents were not there. The king was leading his warriors into battle, and the queen had gone to visit Sybil's grandmother in the next kingdom.

Sybil would have to find the witch herself—in just three days.

The next morning, the princess returned to the forest so early that dew still clung to the grass. She walked for miles, zigzagging and backtracking, peering into caves, behind trees, and under rocks. She tramped through the forest all that day, but she found no trace of the witch's home.

On the second day, the princess searched for anyone who could help. She asked an old woodcutter, a woman who lived in a forest hut, and villagers nearby, but no one knew where to find the Witch of the Woods.

On the third morning, the princess felt desperate. She had only one day left. She wondered if the witch had become an owl again. All day long, Sybil scanned the treetops until her neck ached. She even climbed a huge pine to look out over the forest. But she saw nothing resembling a witch, only squirrels and foxes and every songbird imaginable.

When she had lowered herself almost down to the ground, she saw something suspicious. She held tight to the tree and didn't make a sound. For there below her, a deer was scooting past—but it didn't look quite like a deer. Its eyes glowed like those of the witch.

The moment it ran past, Sybil dropped down from the tree and chased it, staying out of sight as best she could. Several times she almost lost track of it, but finally it stopped by an abandoned well. Sybil peeked around a tree and saw, to her amazement, that the deer was shrinking down to the ground and turning into a little green frog. With one gigantic leap, the frog disappeared into the well.

Sybil heard the splash and rushed over in time to see the frog swim to one side, where there seemed to be an opening. The princess was so eager to follow that she didn't even test the rope that held the bucket. She just climbed in and lowered herself down to the spot where the frog had disappeared. Luckily the old rope held. There on the side of the well she saw a small door—firmly closed—with an iron knocker in the shape of a *scorpion.*

Instantly Sybil knew this must be the place "where the scorpion's voice resounds." She had found the door to the witch's home. She was so excited she almost fell out of the bucket, but she made herself wait until she heard the witch snoring. Then she quickly twisted the iron scorpion off the door and put it into her leather pouch. It was harder to pull herself out of the well than it had been to lower herself in, but she tugged on the rope, hand over hand, until she reached the top. Then she raced back to the castle and hid the iron scorpion under her bed.

At midnight an owl flew out of the moonlit forest. It swooped through the princess's window and landed beside her. Sybil sat up and saw that its eyes were glowing. Much as she wanted to dive under the covers, she watched its head turn hideous and its feathers disappear. The owl became the Witch of the Woods. Sybil had expected her, but she still shrank back.

"You didn't find my home," the witch chortled. "So you and your first love will be mine."

"You're wrong," said Sybil. Her hands were shaking, but she reached under the bed for the iron scorpion. "You live at the bottom of a well."

The witch stamped her foot. "I'll get you yet," she screeched, lunging for the princess with her sinewy arms outstretched. But Sybil was too quick. She threw the iron scorpion at the witch, just as the warmth from her hands brought it to life. It stung one of the witch's gnarled fingers with its poisonous tail. The witch turned into stone and crashed to the floor. The scorpion turned back into iron.

The princess wondered what had brought the scorpion to life. But she finally understood the rest of the witch's clue. Not only did the scorpion's voice resound in the well, the scorpion was bound by the witch's spell—sometimes alive, and sometimes made of iron.

Sybil climbed back into bed. Tomorrow she would get the servants to throw the stone witch into the well. But she decided to keep the scorpion. She tucked it under her pillow, not realizing that the warmth of her body was what brought it to life. As she slept there in her cozy bed, the scorpion began to stir.

Wishes Gone Awry
SCOTLAND

John thought Helen was the prettiest girl in the village, but she had no use for him. "Why would I marry a fisherman like you," she asked, "when I could marry the lord of the manor?"

John strode out of her house and down the steep path to the beach. He was too angry to see the spring flowers bursting into bloom or notice the soft breeze blowing in from the sea. But suddenly he stopped. What was that eerie sound—unlike anything he had ever heard before? It was almost as if the wind and the waves were singing a haunting melody.

He crept along the path. A pebble, loosened by his foot, rattled down to the beach. Did the singer hear him coming? He stood listening—and the unearthly song continued.

When he reached the bottom of the path, he slipped behind a boulder and peeked around one side. The hair at the back of his neck stood on end. There was a stranger there, singing that eerie song. She was half under the waves, tucking seashells and starfish into her long golden curls.

How odd! John thought. But he was even more surprised by what she did next. She swam to the shore and flung herself up on a flat-topped rock—*with a flip of her tail!*

So, mermaids *were* real, just as his grandmother had said so long ago. Her old stories flooded into his mind. "They're a fickle lot," she'd told him. "If they like you, they'll give you calm seas. If they don't like you, expect trouble. But listen. If you find a fishy scale from a mermaid's tail, she must grant you three wishes."

Three wishes? That's just what John needed. He tiptoed over to the mermaid's rock and leaped up behind her, plucking one of her golden scales. She screeched and slapped him with her tail. He waved the scale in front of her nose. "Now you owe me three wishes."

"You didn't find it. You took it," she cried. She tried to grab it back. It was obvious to John that she was furious. Then a crafty look came into her eyes.

"Maybe I could grant your wishes after all," she said in falsely honeyed tones.

"My first wish is for Helen to marry me," he said. "I don't understand why she said no.

"My second wish is to catch the biggest fish in the sea,

so I'll make lots of money and won't have to go fishing every day.

"My third wish is not to die by drowning." He had known too many fishermen whose lives had been lost at sea.

"Granted!" said the mermaid, but this time her voice was harsh. She dove into the waves and swam away, but when she turned to look back at him, he felt a twinge of fear. Her eyes were flashing with anger.

John remembered what his grandmother had said about the amazing powers of mermaids. He began to wonder if he should have plucked that golden scale. Would the angry mermaid unleash a ferocious storm—or send a devastating wave upon the land? And what if she was so mad she didn't grant his wishes after all? He decided to test her word.

John ran up the path to the village and went directly to Helen's house. Again he asked Helen, "Will you marry me?" She looked dumbfounded. The thought in her head was "of course not." But the word that came out of her mouth was "yes."

One wish granted, John said to himself, but what he really should have wished for was a *happy* marriage, because Helen made his life miserable. She didn't understand why she had said yes, and she never stopped telling John how unhappy she was to be his bride. Even the neighbors could hear her screaming at him. He no longer regretted fishing every day. It was such a relief to get out of the house and away from her nagging.

One morning, John decided to see if his second wish would come true. He bought a far stronger fish line than usual and a much bigger hook. Then off he sailed. When he reached a likely spot, he baited the hook, flung out the line, and settled down to wait for a bite from the biggest fish in the sea. "Today's the day," he shouted, hoping that the mermaid was listening.

He was dreaming about how much money he would earn, when his fishing pole was almost jerked out of his hands. It was all John could do to hang on while the fish pulled him and his boat far out to sea.

When the fish leaped out of the water, it looked more like a monster, with gigantic teeth and huge golden scales. Stranger yet, its angry eyes looked very much like those of the mermaid, but magnified one thousand times.

The fish whipped the line first one way, then the other. It circled the boat, again leaping above the waves, then splashing down, drenching John with seawater. The fish looked at least a hundred years old and very likely would taste vile. *Who would want to buy it?* thought John. Even if he managed to pull it aboard, it would sink his boat, so he reluctantly cut his fish line.

But the fish didn't seem very grateful to be free. It spit out the hook and dove deep under the waves. Then it sped upward, smashing the boat to pieces. John was thrown into the water, and the fish began to circle him. Would it swallow him in one gulp? The mermaid hadn't made any promises about that. But the fish finally turned and swam away.

John clutched a plank that had risen to the surface and hugged it to his chest. Hour after hour he floated along. He was burned by the sun and chilled by the waves. His lips cracked and stung, constantly splashed by salty seawater. He almost hoped that the fish would come back and swallow him. *Why*, he asked himself, *did I ever wish to catch such a big fish?*

When the incoming tide finally washed him up on the beach, he realized the mermaid had fulfilled his third wish. She had not let him drown, but he was cold and exhausted and utterly miserable. He staggered to his feet and saw her sitting on the same rock, watching him as she combed her long golden hair. She looked incredibly triumphant. Did it please her that his wishes had gone awry?

John crawled up the path to the village. When he tottered home, Helen started berating him. "What did you do to yourself?" she scolded. He told her all the terrible things he'd endured, but she just screamed, "You lost our boat? Now what will we do?"

John fell into bed without bothering to take off his

clothes and pulled a pillow over his ears. When he awoke, he was ranting about dangerous mermaids.

"Stop blaming mermaids," Helen screeched. "They don't exist!"

John decided he would prove her wrong if it was the last thing he did. He went down to the beach and stayed from sunrise to sunset—day after day—peering around rocks, scanning the waves. He had to catch that mermaid to prove himself to his wife.

One day he hid under a pile of sea grass that had washed in with the tide. He waited there for hours. Bugs dropped out of the grass and crawled all over him. Sand sifted into his hair and ears and down the back of his shirt. At last, the unsuspecting mermaid swam ashore and flipped herself up on the nearest rock. She was singing her haunting songs again—and the longer John listened, the odder he felt.

Before she completely befuddled his mind, John started to inch along, moving the entire pile of grass her way. She didn't notice a thing—not until she tilted down her mirror to admire her golden curls. That's when she saw a startling reflection. John was rising out of the grass, ready to catch her. But she was ready, too. She swung around and swatted his nose with her golden mirror.

"If it's scales you want, you can have them."

John was so surprised that he grabbed his poor nose. But he didn't feel skin. His face seemed to be sprouting scales like those of a fish. John wrenched the mirror out of the mermaid's hand, but before he could see what was happening, he dropped it. His hand had turned into a fin. What was wrong with his legs? He flopped down on the sand. He could hardly breathe. He knew he had to get into the sea. Suddenly he was swimming—and was hungrier than he had ever been in his entire life. He lunged for a worm that he saw dangling in the water. But he didn't see the hook.

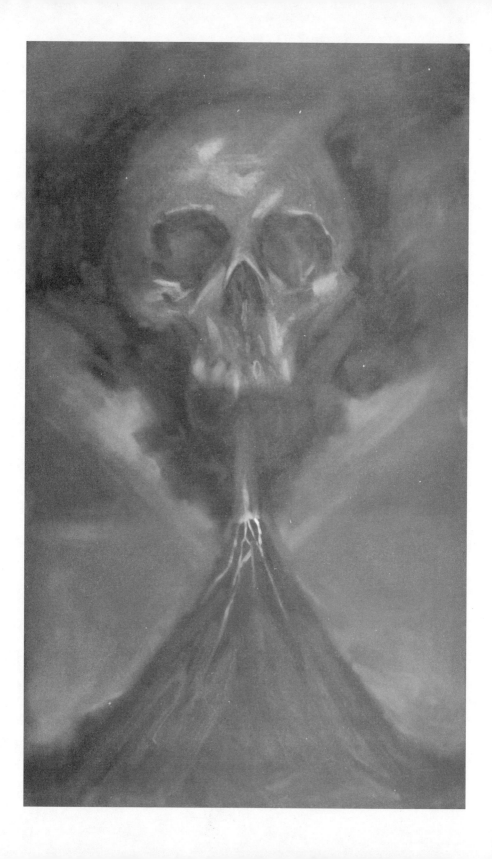

The Ghost of the Rainbow Maiden

HAWAII

Chief Kauhi could be every bit as cruel
as the shark god he worshipped. Yet he wanted rainbows
to arch over his house and the beautiful Rainbow Maiden
to dwell therein.

She refused.

Chief Kauhi was so angry that he killed the Rainbow
Maiden and buried her deep under the roots of a great
koa tree. But he couldn't kill her ghost. It crept out of her
body through the little hole at the corner of her eye, rose
up through the soft dirt, and began to wander about,
invisible to everyone.

The ghost was determined not to go to the underworld.
It wanted to be restored to the Rainbow Maiden's body, so
she could live again.

Whenever anyone came past the koa tree, the ghost
whistled softly, hoping someone would help. But the

whistle sounded like wind rustling through the leaves. The ghost tried brushing the eyelashes of anyone who walked by, making their eyelids tremble. But they merely rubbed their eyes and continued walking.

The ghost began to fear that it would be separated from the body of the Rainbow Maiden forever. It felt the shadow of eternal death descending. But just as it was about to give up hope, a noble chieftain named Mahana sat down to rest, leaning against the trunk of the koa tree. Maybe his love for the Rainbow Maiden had led him there. He had searched everywhere else. Or maybe he was particularly aware of ghosts. After all, two spirit sisters, disguised as real women, protected his family.

Suddenly he felt his hand quivering. The ghost of the Rainbow Maiden had touched it. He heard the sound of leaves rustling overhead, but there was no wind. As the ghost hovered around him, he felt its anguish.

He jumped up and circled the tree. There on the other side was freshly dug soil. He dropped to his knees and began digging frantically with his hands. He tore aside the roots of the koa tree and kept digging until he came upon a fearsome sight—the bruised body of the Rainbow Maiden. It was still warm.

Mahana raced home with the body, calling to his witch doctor for help. But all their prayers and rituals did not work. The Rainbow Maiden's body and ghost did not reunite. Had they been separated too long?

Mahana sought help again. This time he called to the ghost sisters who watched over his family's welfare. Somehow, as fellow ghosts, they brought the ghost of the Rainbow Maiden closer to her body. Then, while the witch doctor chanted, they pushed that spirit into the maiden's feet and slowly up her body until it was restored to its rightful home. Under the tender care of Mahana and the ghost sisters, the Rainbow Maiden recovered her health.

But Mahana feared that the maiden was in great danger. If Chief Kauhi learned of her whereabouts, he would kill her again.

The Rainbow Maiden loved Mahana, but she couldn't stand living hidden from the world. She wanted to play in the mists, spreading arcs of color across the sky.

Mahana decided he must find a way to challenge and defeat Chief Kauhi. So Mahana went out to look for him. He found him surfing on a gigantic wave, pleasing his shark god and showing off for his family.

"What makes you think you are so brave?" Mahana taunted. "A child could surf that wave."

Chief Kauhi left the water and strode up the beach. He thrust his face close to Mahana's. "You don't know how brave I am. I've even killed someone."

"Who?" demanded Mahana.

"The Rainbow Maiden," bragged the chief.

Mahana jumped at the chance to call him a liar. "You didn't kill her," he said. "She still lives."

Chief Kauhi was furious. "You are the liar!" he said. "She must be a ghost who has taken on human form. I'll prove it."

"And what if you can't?"

"If I am wrong, I'll leap into the volcano. But if I am right, *you* will leap in!"

Mahana accepted the challenge so quickly that Chief Kauhi began to worry. He hurried home to tell his own witch doctor that they must devise a test for ghosts.

"We'll outwit her," said his evil witch doctor. "We'll place large and delicate leaves on the path that the Rainbow Maiden must walk upon. The judges will notice that her feet do not bruise or tear the leaves. They will know that she walks as lightly as a ghost."

The fateful day arrived. All was ready for the sacrifice. Crowds began to come from all parts of the island.

When the Rainbow Maiden approached, the spirit sisters were still guarding her. They immediately knew that the path of delicate leaves was a test for ghosts. The maiden could pass the test, but they could not. If anyone discovered that they were ghosts, the spirit-catchers would seize them and take them to the depths of the underworld.

"You must crush the leaves on both sides as you move along," they told the Rainbow Maiden, "so we can fool the judges as we walk beside you."

The Maiden quietly bruised and broke a wide swath of leaves as she passed through the crowds. The judges were convinced that she was human.

But Chief Kauhi refused to be defeated so easily. "I feel the presence of ghosts around her," he shouted. "They must be punished." He proposed yet another method of ghost testing before he himself was sacrificed.

"Bring forth a calabash of water," he told his witch doctor. "You can tell if ghosts are reflected there."

His witch doctor filled the gourd and tried to wait patiently. But in his eagerness to serve his evil chief, he leaned forward for a better view and saw his own reflection there. His spirit had escaped from his body and was bathing in the water. Mahana leaped forward, plunged his hands into the water, and crushed the spirit face before it could leap back into the doctor's body. The witch doctor fell dead before he could detect reflections of ghosts—and the spirit sisters were spared.

And Chief Kauhi? He tried to run away. But the crowd blocked his escape. They marched the murderous chieftain up the slope of the volcano. When he neared the brink, he suddenly lunged for Mahana.

"You'll share my fate," the chief shouted, rushing toward Mahana to knock him into the volcano. But Mahana twisted away, falling to the ground.

The chief tripped on Mahana's leg, plunged over the edge, and fell screaming into the fiery cauldron.

The Wife's Tale
CHINA

It was long past bedtime when a Chinese trader arrived in town. He dismounted from his mule and knocked halfheartedly at a few doors. He hated to awaken anyone in the middle of the night. So he walked back and forth, wondering what to do. But just as he passed a tumble-down house, an old man stepped out.

"We would be honored if you stayed with us," he said, "if you don't mind eating cold food that's a day old."

Well, the trader was relieved to find any sort of shelter at all. He tied his mule to a handy tree and followed the old man indoors.

Oddly enough, there was no furniture in sight. The old man scurried about, first bringing in a low bench, then a low table, and then a bowl of rice with a few scraps of meat.

The old man apologized for serving such a humble

meal, but the trader barely listened, because he saw the man's lovely daughter enter the room with a pot of tea.

She didn't behave like most maidens, who lowered their eyes and glanced sideways at strangers. Her dark eyes were fixed directly on the trader. He was surprised but intrigued. What sort of maiden was she? She was quick to refill his cup and to bring more rice. By the time he had finished his meal, he had decided to ask her father's permission to marry her. "May I hope that you will unite our two families?"

"With pleasure," said the old man. "If you will share your house, we will come to live with you."

The next day, the trader returned home to make the necessary arrangements. When all was ready, he rode back to the maiden's town, but before he reached her home, he found her walking down the road. She was dressed in mourning clothes, carrying a bundle, and weeping.

"My father was killed when the back wall of the house fell on him," she said. "I must bury him today. Please wait for me here."

"Can't I help you?" he asked, reaching for her bundle.

"Not if you love me," she said. As she twisted away, he felt something brush against his wrist that felt like cats' whiskers. The maiden quickly pulled the wrapping tight around the bundle, sobbing harder than ever. When she disappeared into a clump of trees, she was still cradling the bundle in her arms.

What was happening? The trader leaned against a tree, confused and impatient, but he waited until she returned— with no bundle in hand.

"Now we must sell our grain," she said, leading him back to her house. When they had found enough buyers to empty the granary, she gathered up her things, and the trader helped her onto his mule.

The maiden did not complain about the long and tiring ride, but she did make a strange request. "Never speak to my old neighbors about me or my father. They are a bad lot," she said. No matter how many times the trader asked her why, she would not say.

When they reached the trader's home, they were warmly welcomed by his parents and his brother. Soon a lucky day was chosen for the marriage, and the trader and his bride began a happy life together. She spent much of her time spinning, earning money for her new family. She also brought them good fortune. Their granary seemed to remain full no matter how much they ate.

One day the trader's brother happened to travel to the very town where his sister-in-law once lived. He didn't know that he should not mention her to her old neighbors. So he told them how his brother had been welcomed into the house next door to theirs.

"You must be mistaken," said the neighbor. "No one has lived in that house for years. Something frightened the owners away. Then the back wall fell in. When I heard the noise, I went over. Do you know what I saw buried under the rubble? Something big and furry." His voice dropped so low that his words were muffled. "It wasn't moving." He leaned closer. "But when I looked minutes later, it had *disappeared*. I'll never go near that house again."

The trader's brother was amazed. When he returned home, he took his brother aside and told him what the neighbor had said.

"No one lived there?" cried the trader. "How can you believe such rumors? Now I know why she said the neighbors were a bad lot." But as much as he loved his wife, he began to watch her closely for strange signs.

He noticed how she sniffed the food she was cooking. "Only to make sure I have flavored it well," she said. He also noticed that her teeth were growing longer. One night he was awakened by a gnawing sound. He arose and startled his wife, who dropped a piece of wood on the floor. "I have a bad toothache," she said. "This numbs the pain." But she seemed upset that he had seen her gnawing wood.

What worried him most was the way she sometimes disappeared at night. He often heard scurrying around the granary. Was she scavenging grain from surrounding farms?

One night he went out to investigate and saw a large rat with an unusually long tail. It was carrying a small sack of grain in its teeth. At first it cowered, looking straight at

him with dark, beady eyes. But when the trader tried to kill it with a big stick, the rat defended itself. It jumped onto the trader's back and bit his neck. He dropped his stick and swatted the rat with his hands—giving it the opportunity it needed to flee. But it limped as it raced away.

The next morning, the trader's neck was swollen and sore. His wife moistened towels with cool water and held them against the wound to reduce the swelling.

The trader was torn between love and fear. Was he imagining things, or was his wife limping? And what was that bruise, mostly hidden by the sleeve of her robe? He was desperate to know what was happening, so he tried something drastic. He brought a ferocious cat into the household. His wife didn't say anything, but there was fear in her eyes when she watched it bite off the head of a mouse.

The next morning, his wife's face and hands were bandaged, and the cat's ear was bitten. "That cat attacked me," she cried. "Please take it away!"

Now her husband was more suspicious than ever, but he was sorry to see his wife suffering, so he put the cat outdoors.

That night, the trader heard wild caterwauling. It sounded like alley cats fighting over tidbits of food. When he saw that his wife was not in bed, he rushed outside. An army of cats raced away, led by the ferocious mouser. The trader looked down at his feet, horrified. There on the doorstep was an unusually long rat's tail and scraps of rat fur.

Where was his wife? She was nowhere to be found.

Youth without Age
TURKEY

Even before the prince entered the world, he drove his parents wild. "I never knew that babies could scream before they were born," groaned the king. "Nor I," sobbed the queen. At least the king could leave the room. But the poor queen had no relief, day or night, from the little one screaming inside her.

The greatest magicians in the land were summoned. They tried their most powerful spells. They sang and they chanted before the pregnant queen. But nothing silenced the screaming.

The king tried promises. "My darling child," he said, "I will give you all the kingdoms east of the sun and west of the moon." Still the baby screamed. "If you are a boy, I will find you a bride as lovely as the Fairy Queen. If you are a girl, you will be wed to the finest prince in the land." The baby screamed even louder.

The king grew desperate. "I will give you *Youth without Age* and *Life without Death*," he declared. Only then did the screaming stop—and shortly thereafter a baby boy entered the world. During his son's childhood, the king didn't think twice about the extravagant promise he had made.

The prince was a remarkably calm child. He no longer screamed or even raised his voice. His smiles brightened the lives of everyone in the castle. But on his sixteenth birthday, his mood changed. He stood before his father, looking unusually determined. "It's time," he said, "for you to give me what you promised before I was born."

The king turned pale. "How can I give you something the world has never known? I only wished to quiet you."

"Then I must seek it for myself," said the prince. The king and the queen were brokenhearted. How could they let their beloved son set forth on such an unlikely quest? Where could he possibly find Life without Death? They warned him of the dangers he would face. They told him that if he stayed, he soon would rule the kingdom himself. They begged and they pleaded, but he would not listen.

Finally the king said, "If you must go, I want you to take my strongest horse." The prince raced down to his father's stables. How could he choose among such handsome chargers? His father had the finest in all the land. But something odd happened when the prince touched them. They trembled. It was almost as if the horses knew the dangers of the prince's quest.

Only one horse stood steady. That was the one the prince chose—a worthy companion for his long journey. He told his servants to saddle it while he said good-bye to the king and the queen.

"You must take my warriors with you," said the king. But the prince wanted to find his destiny by himself, so he soon ordered them to return home. He did not know what dangers lay ahead, but he trusted himself and his horse.

He rode for days and weeks and months, until he came to a land so far away that nothing seemed familiar. When he stopped by a hut to see if he could spend the night, a five-eyed witch came to the door. She spit fire and flame and threatened to burn the prince to a cinder.

"Cook my dinner, instead," he demanded.

The witch was startled. Why didn't he flee? She had never met such a brave man before. "Wait," she said. "If you gather some wood, I will light a fire."

But the moment he rode off to look for wood, the witch turned herself into a beautiful maiden. She turned her hut into a palace and moved it farther into the forest. She knew the prince would travel that way. "Welcome," she said, when he rode up to the castle door. He was holding an armload of wood and looking lost. "Come right in."

Before the prince knew it, he found himself enchanted

by the maiden and her spells. The prince spent a happy
week with her. He fed apples to the unicorns that she summoned to the lawn each morning. He shared the splendid
meals that magically appeared on her table. And when he
climbed to the castle roof with her, he saw more falling
stars in a single night than he had seen in his entire life-
time. But a witch is a witch at heart, and she soon tired of
being pleasant.

"Off you go," she said, still looking like a maiden but
beginning to spit a little fire.

The prince raced away on his horse, his mind confused by the witch's spells. He didn't understand that he must remain with the witch if he hoped to fulfill his quest. All he knew was that he had an unbearable yearning to see his parents. He *must* return home.

But as he rode back, he discovered that forests had become fields, and villages had turned to cities. When the prince asked how this could have happened in the short week he was gone, people scurried away. They looked back over their shoulders, frightened by his wild eyes and his old-fashioned clothing.

This made the prince so angry that he didn't notice that his hair had turned white, as well as his beard. As he rode along, his legs began to tremble and his beard grew all the way down to his waist. His horse began to falter. He didn't realize that the seven days he had spent with the witch really were seven hundred years.

When he reached his parents' palace, all that he saw was ruin and weeds. The prince searched every corner of every room. He looked through every stall in the stable. But he found that nothing from his childhood remained. Finally he pushed aside rubble and went down to the palace cellar. By now his beard was flapping against his knees and he could barely totter along. All he found there was a battered strongbox.

The prince struggled to lift the lid. Inside he saw something that looked like a shriveled leaf. But to his horror, it rose up and spoke. "Had you left me here much longer, I would have perished," said his Death.

Its withered hand reached out and touched the prince. Instantly, he crumbled into dust. His quest for Youth without Age and Life without Death had failed.

The Haunted Violin

GERMANY

Even the magician couldn't stop the passage of time. When his long life was about to end, he asked a carpenter to make his coffin. "Use wood from this tree," he said, pointing to one that shaded his doorstep. "It sprang from the ground the day I was born. Be sure to use it for my coffin . . . and for nothing else."

For nothing else? This seemed strange to the carpenter. But he was even more surprised when the magician said, "Treat the wood gently. Take care not to make it cry."

The carpenter couldn't imagine a tree crying, but he wanted to make the coffin, so he agreed to do exactly what the magician asked. He listened hard when he felled the tree and cut it into boards, but he heard nothing unusual. No crying—unless the wood's voice was muffled by the sound of his saw.

When the old magician died, the carpenter sanded boards for the coffin. He saw that the wood was magnificent, dark and straight grained. It was much too lovely to bury under the dirt.

The carpenter couldn't decide what to do. Should he use the wood as he pleased? Or should he honor the magician's wish? In the end he reluctantly used the wood for the coffin and delivered it in time for the magician's burial.

When he returned to his workshop, the carpenter stared at the few boards that were left over. *Surely the magician wouldn't want them to go to waste,* he thought. *They would make an excellent violin. I'll start working on it tomorrow.*

That night, however, the old magician burst into his dreams. *"Don't you dare use my wood for a violin,"* he said. *"Don't do it!"* The carpenter awoke. He lay there thinking for a moment, but he never paid attention to dreams. Besides, he was tired, so he turned over and went back to sleep.

The very next day, he began carving the wood. He labored over it for weeks until he had made an elegant violin—handsomely shaped and beautifully polished. He could hardly wait to hear how it sounded. But, in order to play it, he had to make a bow. *I'll begin first thing in the morning,* he told himself.

That night the dead magician returned. *"Now you have*

done it!" he told the carpenter. "*And it will be much worse if you make a bow.*" The carpenter was feeling a bit uneasy when he awoke, but again he dismissed his dream. He worked hard all day, shaping and varnishing the bow. But he couldn't try it out until morning, when the varnish had dried.

He went to bed, and again he dreamed about the magician. The dead man was very angry. "*This is your last chance,*" he said. "*Do not play that violin!*"

The next morning, the carpenter felt a twinge of fear. But he knew that nothing had happened when he had finished making the violin. Why should he worry about playing it? He hurried to his workshop, strung the bow, took down the violin, and began to play. He was not a skilled violinist, so he was astounded by the haunting melody that arose. It seemed to spring forth on its own, crying like a dirge sung at a funeral.

But no sooner had he finished playing than the room turned dark. He rushed to the window and leaned out to see if the sun had been eclipsed, but all he saw was more darkness.

Suddenly invisible hands picked him up and thrust him out the window. The carpenter tumbled down and sank into something soft. He realized with horror that it was quicksand, sucking him into the earth. He thrashed about wildly, but it was too late. The quicksand dragged him under as he drew his last breath.

When the carpenter's son entered the workshop later that morning, he found his father's body lying on the floor

with the violin clutched in his hands. The son was distraught. He didn't know what had happened. But that night, the same magician visited the son's dreams to tell him what had taken place.

The son awoke, confused. What sort of magic was in that tree? One thing the son knew for sure—that violin was dangerous. He arose at dawn and burned it. As it went up in flames, he thought he heard a voice crying out from afar. Was the soul of the carpenter being tortured somewhere? Or was that the voice of the magician, crying out from his grave?

The Evil Sea Ghost
NORWAY

"Beware of draugs," an old fisherman warned Jack, "or you'll sink beneath the waves."

Jack barely listened. He'd heard that draugs were ghosts of men lost at sea—men who were not buried in the churchyard. But Jack had never seen one.

"Some have no heads at all," said the old fisherman. His voice dropped to a whisper. "But the worst have heads of seaweed, with slimy green teeth as sharp as nails. Beware if you hear them at night, barging around the boathouse."

Jack looked hard at the old man. Did he know that Jack had heard strange noises the evening before? Wasn't it rats? Of course it was rats, Jack told himself.

The old fisherman moved closer. "If a draug gets into the boathouse," he whispered, "expect foul weather. If it comes aboard, you'll be shipwrecked. But that's not the worst. If it sails alongside you in a halfboat, prepare to die."

The old man's tales might have frightened Jack when he was a boy. But now he was twenty. He had no time for such talk. He needed to earn money for his widowed mother and his younger sister and brothers. So he went fishing each morning—and today he was late.

Jack nodded politely to the old man and set sail. Sunlight sparkled on the waves. Jack headed for one of his favorite spots, close to craggy rocks jutting out of the sea. But before he had a chance to bait his hooks, clouds rolled in—dark, menacing clouds. Soon gentle waves turned into huge swells, and the wind began to howl. Jack knew he must sail home.

How could a storm rise so quickly? Towering waves threatened to swamp Jack's boat. He held the rudder with one hand and frantically bailed with the other. Sails whipped in the wind, and rain poured down his face.

Oh for a better boat, Jack thought, one that would ride high and light, skimming across the sea.

That's when a rogue wave—bigger than all the rest—flipped the boat and flung Jack overboard. He struggled to the surface and clawed his way onto the upturned hull. He grasped the keel with his hands and held tight with his knees.

The billowing waves drenched him. Chills shook his

body. He thrust his sheaf knife into the wooden hull and clung to it. His hands were numb. Would his fingers slip? Would he ever see his family again?

The words of the old fisherman rang in his head. *"If a draug gets into the boathouse, expect foul weather."*

Suddenly Jack realized it *was* a draug he had heard in the boathouse the evening before. Not rats! That evil ghost was just waiting to brew up a storm. Jack wished he'd heeded the old fisherman's warning. He would never doubt him again.

When Jack had almost lost hope, he heard the surf hitting the rocky shore. He glimpsed his own dock through sheets of rain and realized that the tide was slowly carrying him home. He willed himself to hang on a little longer, pressing his numbed knees hard against the wood.

It seemed like an eternity to Jack, but finally the sea flung him onto land. He crawled up to his boathouse, too weak to reach his own bed, and burrowed beneath a pile of old sails. He went to sleep wondering if draugs were lurking nearby.

By the next morning he was sick with a high fever and bone-rattling chills. His mind began to wander. He imagined hearing draugs—under the floor, in the attic, everywhere. He howled and shouted, but he refused to leave the boathouse.

Only his little sister, Malfri, wasn't afraid of him. She skipped down to the boathouse each day with a pail of food their mother had prepared—loaves of bread, cheese, and fish liver covered with molasses. When he began to recover, he made toys for Malfri. But if others came near, he still howled. He wanted to be left alone so he could work—for he had vowed never to go to sea again until he had a safer boat. And how would he get it? He would have to build it himself.

Jack drew plans for the sleekest boat in all of Norway. Wood shavings and sawdust piled up around his feet. But no matter how many times he shaped each plank, nothing fit. He redrew his plans and redid his work, but still it didn't please him. He labored endlessly, barely sleeping.

One night he took a catnap, curled up on a pile of shavings. He dreamed that he had finished his boat and was out sailing when a draug clambered aboard. Planks began to splinter, water rushed in, and the boat sank to the bottom of the sea.

Jack awoke drenched with sweat, his eyes wild. He lit a lantern and looked once more at his unfinished boat. It seemed hopelessly twisted and misshapen. He grabbed a cowbell and threw it at the boat. It rang violently.

"Did you call me?" asked an unearthly voice. A cold wind from the sea blew in the window.

Jack saw an awful draug slip out of the shadows and sit down on his boat. The ghost was dripping water and grinning, revealing its pointed green teeth.

Jack flung a pail at it. The pail went right through the draug, hit the wall, and bounced back. Jack ducked, terrified. Why had the draug come to the boathouse? What did it want? Was it about to unleash another storm?

"No storms," the draug hissed, reading his mind, "only a proposition. You can build the finest boats in all of Norway, if . . ." And it lingered for a moment, looking incredibly evil. "If you will let me set the keel in place, with all its flaws, in every seventh boat. If you want a sea boat, you must accept a death boat."

Before Jack could utter a word, the draug beckoned to him. "Come see," it said, leading Jack out to the water's edge. An unbelievably sleek new boat was moored there. Jack had never seen the likes of it, nor had anyone else.

"If you want to build such boats," the draug said, "knock three times on the keel before the sun rises. But I must tell you that you cannot stop building them once you start."

Jack tested the boat, rocking it with his foot, amazed to see how lightly it rode upon the water. He knocked twice, then stopped before the fateful third knock. How could he accept such an evil proposition?

"Why not take the chance?" asked the draug, and it disappeared into the water without a splash.

Jack ran his hand along the smooth planks, admiring the perfect workmanship and the seaworthy design. Again he knocked twice, and again he stopped.

He headed back to the boathouse, arguing with himself. But then he saw his own ungainly, unfinished boat. With an anguished howl, he raced back to the water's edge—and he knocked on the keel . . . once . . . twice . . . three times.

Instantly the draug rose out of the water. "Remember," it hissed. "In every seventh boat, *I* will set the keel." Then the draug vanished, and so did the boat.

Most of that night Jack lay awake. But just before the sun rose, he told himself, *What's done is done,* and he fell into a fitful sleep.

The next morning, Jack tore apart the boat he was building and began again. This time his hands took over. His saws cut cleanly, and every plank molded itself into place.

Before long, Jack was ready to launch his beautiful boat. It sailed like a seabird, wondrous to watch. But how could he enjoy it? No sooner had he set sail than he was anxious to return to the boathouse. He *must* build more boats.

Luckily many fishermen wanted boats like Jack's, so he no longer needed to fish for his family. He became a boat builder, and the money rolled in.

It seemed to Jack that each new boat he built was more beautiful than the last. And the seventh boat? That was the loveliest of all.

In those days there was a bailiff who imposed harsh taxes on fishermen and farmers alike. When he heard about Jack's success, he headed straight to the boathouse.

"You haven't been paying your taxes," he shouted at Jack. "I'll throw you in prison for the rest of your life. You'll rot in a dark cell. You'll never see your family again . . . unless . . ." and he eyed Jack's seventh boat . . . "unless you give me that boat."

Little Malfri cried when the bailiff took Jack's lovely boat. But Jack laughed so hard he could barely speak. "No one," he gasped, "deserves it more."

That fall he heard the news. The boat had taken the bailiff to the bottom of the sea.

Jack built so many boats that he stopped counting. He no longer knew which was a seventh boat. He told himself not to worry—he was saving far more lives than he was losing.

One Sunday, Jack's family sailed across the bay to church. It was faster to go by boat than to take the long road that curved around the shore. Jack stayed home. He wanted to finish the new hull he was building. He heard the wind rise. Soon it was whistling through the cracks in the old boathouse. All day the storm grew stronger.

Night fell. Why hadn't his family returned? He swept some wood shavings aside, telling himself that his boats could ride out any weather.

The wind turned even wilder, shaking the boathouse. Jack listened to it howl. But then he heard something else. It sounded like voices moaning outside the boathouse door—and fingernails clawing at the latch.

"Begone," he shouted, thinking some strange creature had risen from the sea. But the scratching and moaning continued.

The door flew open. There was Malfri clinging to Jack's mother. There were his brothers. All were dripping wet, pale and gray, with horror written on their faces, their eyes staring at nothing.

"Give back my life," moaned Malfri.

Jack rushed down to his boat and sailed into the storm, looking for his family. But all he found was a death boat, bottom side up, with a gaping hole in its keel.

He began to sob. "What have I done?"

Jack tried to lose himself in his work. But the moment he stopped sawing and hammering, the voices of his family returned. The moaning of Malfri was the worst to bear.

Bony fishermen began to rise out of the sea and search for Jack, reaching for him with their skeletal hands. He could no longer sleep.

He desperately wanted to know which of his boats were the death boats. He tested those stored in the boat-house, thumping the keels, searching for flaws. But he could find none. He no longer thought his boats were beautiful.

Even moonlight shining on the waves gave him no pleasure. For it let him see ghostly crews wading through the shallows—and as they came closer, the stench of rot was almost unbearable.

He shouted, "Many more would have drowned if I hadn't built my boats. Go away!" But they swarmed around him, staring at him with their hollow eyes.

Jack was frantic. He fled in one of his boats, sailing out to sea.

He could barely stand looking at the broken planks floating by, pieces of boats, all green and slimy. Bony fingers reached out of the water and tried to grasp them, then slipped from sight.

Jack's boat skimmed through the waves, but it was not

as seaworthy as it seemed. For it was not Jack who had set its keel in place.

That was the work of the evil draug.

Suddenly the draug appeared again, keeping pace with Jack as it sailed beside him. Jack was horrified to see that the back half of the draug's boat was missing. He turned pale. He could almost hear what the old fisherman had whispered so long ago. *"If it sails alongside you in a halfboat, prepare to die."*

"Begone!" Jack shouted at the draug—as if he could change his fate.

But the keel of Jack's boat started creaking and cracking and falling away. Water rushed in through a gaping hole, flooding the boat.

The last thing that Jack saw, before he sank beneath the waves, was the draug, grinning monstrously, licking its pointed green teeth.

The Peasants' Revenge
GERMANY

The peasants were terrified of Lord Hatto. Whenever he rode past, women dropped their loads of wood and darted through the nearest doorways. Children ran alongside mothers, hiding behind their skirts. Men hurried to cultivate the far sides of fields to avoid Hatto's stinging whip. Even cats fled. No one knew when Hatto would unleash one of his towering rages.

The peasants wished he would be punished for his evil ways. But who dared to challenge such a powerful lord?

The only things that pleased Hatto were money and food. He spent hours counting his bags full of coins—and even more hours eating. The moment he rushed down the castle stairs each morning, he began bellowing for smoked eels and blackbird pies. Then more eels—and more pies. Finally, when he could not eat another bite, he pushed his vast body away from the table. He scowled when servants were slow to drape a cloak over his shoulders, grabbed his whip, and stomped off to his stables.

Pity the poor groom who did not have the lord's horse saddled and waiting—and pity the poor horse, ridden by such a harsh and heavy master.

Each day, Hatto rode to his bulging granaries to inspect the locks. He wanted to make sure his peasants had not taken even a handful of his wheat to feed their hungry children. Of course the peasants had grown the wheat, but they had grown it on Hatto's land, so Hatto claimed almost all of it for himself.

One day, when he was sure that his wheat was untouched, Hatto rode down the steep hillside to the Rhine River. He called across the water to a servant tending the stone tower on an island midstream.

"Did you stop every boat?" he bellowed. "Did you collect my tolls?" The servant nodded his head vigorously. He dared not fail. Imagine Hatto's fury if even one boat slipped by without paying for the privilege.

The lord spent the rest of the day hunting. He would never dirty his hands raising crops—that's what peasants were for—but he enjoyed killing game for his table, especially little songbirds for his steaming pies.

When Hatto rode back to his castle, he whipped his horse into a gallop. It was time to eat, and he knew the cook was roasting the carcass of a young ox.

But when he burst into the kitchen, the cook muffled a shriek and tried to hide something behind his back. It was a kitten. Worse yet, it was chewing a scrap of meat.

"How dare you?" shouted Hatto. He kicked the kitten out the door. "I don't need any more mouths to feed." He almost struck the cook as well. "You know I hate cats," he snarled. But the savory smell of roast ox sent him rushing to the table.

By the time he went to bed, a heavy rain was falling. It rained the next day, too, and the next week, and the next month. In fact, no one could remember a wetter, colder spring. Seed rotted in the ground. Pastures were flooded. Farm animals grew thin.

The peasants soon ate their meager stores of food. Their vegetable gardens were sodden and bare. They begged the lord for wheat, but he refused. So they went to the forests to dig up edible roots and plants. They grew gaunt while the lord continued to feast.

Finally the peasants decided they must approach the lord together. Surely a starving crowd could persuade him to share his wheat.

When Hatto saw them gathering outside the castle door, he was angry. He saw no reason to help his peasants. Why did they keep pestering him? He was about to stomp back into his castle when a sly smile suddenly lit up his face. "Of course," he said. "Come to the granary with me."

The peasants were overjoyed. Maybe the lord would give them enough wheat to save their lives. Hatto unlocked one of his granaries and urged everyone inside. They were surprised to see that the granary was empty. The lord had sold the wheat for outrageous prices when everyone became desperate for food.

The peasants were even more surprised when Hatto suddenly slammed the door shut and bolted it. They cried out, begging for their freedom.

"They sound like a bunch of squealing mice, don't they?" scoffed the lord.

"Squealing mice?" echoed a frightened servant. He dared not disagree, but when Hatto told him to set the granary on fire, he fled in terror. So the lord threw the torches himself. Flames began to lick up the granary walls.

Hatto imagined the peasants suffering horrible, lingering deaths. But only part of his evil wish was fulfilled. There was death, but no suffering. Before the flames touched the peasants, an enormous bolt of lightning ripped down from the heavens. In an instant it destroyed the building and reduced everyone inside to ash.

Lord Hatto was knocked flat on his back. As he lay there, stunned, he watched a vast cloud of ashes rise into the sky. Then the cloud swirled and darkened and began drifting back to earth. He shook his head, blinking. He couldn't believe what he saw. The ashes were clumping together and turning into mice, thousands of huge, squealing mice with razor-sharp teeth and appetites far greater than Hatto's.

He staggered to his feet as mice rained down upon him. Each time he batted one away, ten more struck him, clawing at his clothes as they fell. He raced into the castle with the sea of mice nipping at his heels. So many swarmed through the kitchen door, he couldn't close it. No servants were there to help. All had fled when he set the granary afire.

While the mice paused in the kitchen to eat Hatto's great stores of food, he charged up the stairs. He bolted his bedroom door and jumped into bed. But even when he pulled the covers over his head, he could not escape the sounds of scampering feet, gnawing teeth, and unearthly squeals.

For once in his life, he wished he had been kinder. Not to the peasants, of course. He still was as hard-hearted as ever. But he did wish he had been kinder to cats—to mouse-eating cats.

He lay awake all night, listening to scurrying and squeaking from all corners of the castle. He heard the mice move from the kitchen to the great hall, where they climbed up the walls to chew on tapestries and family portraits. Finally they clambered up the stairs to gnaw holes through Hatto's bedroom door.

By the time the sun rose, they were swarming into the bedroom and shredding the very blankets under which Hatto was hiding.

The lord raced out of the castle and lumbered down the hillside to the Rhine. The mice weren't far behind. He leaped into a boat and started rowing. *I'll be safe on the island,* he told himself. *No mouse would swim across the river.*

Nevertheless, he bolted the door of the stone tower and climbed to its topmost room. He looked down from the window. What was that scum he saw on the surface of the water? It seemed to be moving toward the island.

As it came closer, he began to tremble. It wasn't scum. It was a mass of mice—all swimming his way.

Hatto rushed to the door of the tower room, slammed it shut, and bolted it. Then he barricaded it with bags of money—tolls collected from boat captains. But the doors of the tower were made of wood, and the teeth of the mice were sharp.

Even when he pressed his hands over his ears he could hear the horrendous gnawing at the door below. Wood splintered. Toothy, whiskered faces punched through ever-widening holes. Hoards of mice scampered up the tower stairs, sniffing for blood.

Hatto crouched in a corner, whimpering, "Kitty, kitty, kitty," but none came. The gnawing grew closer, the squeals deafening, and the mice, crazed by hunger, soon poured into the room.

Later that morning, the toll collector rowed out to the island. He could scarcely believe what he saw. The tower

doors were full of ragged holes. Ashes were scattered everywhere. He was tempted to jump back into his boat, but he
gathered up his courage, climbed the stairs, and peeked
into the tower room.

There he saw a few flecks of blood and bone, scattered
over bags of money. Nothing more.

The Wizard's Apprentice

EASTERN EUROPE

A man stood by a fork in the path, try-
ing to decide which way to turn. If he went to the right, he
would reach the hut of a fearsome wizard. If he went to the
left, he would go home to a weeping wife.

He sat down on a stump and put his head in his hands.
Which way should he turn? For weeks his wife had begged
him to seek the wizard's help.

"How else will we ever have a child?" she'd cried. "We've
waited so long. Only magic can help us." But he wasn't so
sure.

He didn't like anything about the wizard—particularly
not what he'd heard in the marketplace that morning. An
old woman had tugged at his sleeve. He had tried to hurry
away, but she insisted on telling him how the wizard had
squashed her husband under his heel.

"How could he do that?" the man had asked.

"First he turned him into an ant."

An ant? The man had shuddered. Could this be true? He'd heard about her husband's disappearance, but was this the work of the wizard?

The woman's story was so upsetting that the man had quickly left the marketplace, and now he was sitting on the stump by the fork in the path. He was still talking to himself, still trying to decide which way to go. He knew how desperately his wife longed for a baby. And, if the truth were known, he did, too. But did he want to face an evil wizard?

Finally the man straightened his shoulders, rose from the stump, and began to walk down the path toward the wizard's hut. An insistent voice inside him kept saying, "Turn around. Go back." But he forced himself onward. The trees grew thicker and the forest darker.

At last he found himself standing in front of the wizard's hut. But even before he had a chance to knock, the wizard suddenly materialized on the doorstep. The man leaped back, almost falling over his feet.

"So," said the wizard. "I understand you want a child."

The man was astounded. How did the wizard know?

"Of course, I know," said the wizard. "Why else would you come to see me?"

The man was about to turn and run. He was terrified that the wizard could read his mind. But before the man could escape, the wizard stretched his arm to twice its normal length and grabbed him. "Come right in," he said, pulling him into the hut.

When the man stepped inside, he almost fainted. What incredible power did this wizard have? From the outside, his hut looked as if it were about to collapse. But from the inside it appeared to be the throne room of a palace. Silk tapestries hung on the walls, and the furniture was made of gold.

"Don't be so surprised," said the wizard. "I have the power to do anything. I can even give you a child. But what can you do for me?" He looked cold and cunning. "How *will* you repay me?"

The man didn't know what to say. He didn't want to offend the wizard by offering a small reward. He felt in his pocket for coins, but he found only three. Not enough.

"You're right," said the wizard, "I would never give you a child for a few coins. Not even for a basketful."

"I could cut firewood for you," the man said, "for a whole year."

"What for?" scoffed the wizard. With a snap of his fingers he made a rock in the fireplace burst into flame, sending waves of heat into the room.

The wizard thought again. "So . . . you'll do something for me for a year?" His face twisted into an evil grin. "I'll make a bargain with you. I'll help you and your wife have a son. But on his tenth birthday you must bring him to me, to serve me for a year. After that you can take him back.

But if you do not bring him to me on his tenth birthday, I'll fetch him myself—then it won't be so easy to regain your son."

"I'll bring him," said the man, too happy about the promise of a child to worry about the wizard's demands.

He said good-bye and whistled all the way home. Not only did he have wonderful news for his wife, he hadn't been turned into an ant.

His wife was so happy when he told her about the child, he didn't mention the wizard's bargain.

Just nine months later, his wife gave birth to a fine baby boy. He was the joy of his parents' lives, with his quick mind and his warm smile. His early years sped past, and it wasn't until the approach of his tenth birthday that the boy's father remembered the wizard's warning.

He hated to admit to his wife that he had agreed to such a terrible bargain, and when he finally did, she wept. "I can't give up our son for a year. You must not take him to the wizard."

"It might be worse if I don't," he said. "This way, at least we will get him back." But she was so miserable that her husband didn't know what to do. In the end he did nothing.

So there they were, sitting at the table on the boy's tenth birthday, eating their supper. They didn't realize that the wizard was peering at them in his magic mirror, furious that they had not set forth.

By the time they finished eating, the sun had gone down. It was much too late to venture into the woods—and that's when it happened. One moment the boy was sitting at the table and the next moment he was flying out the open window . . . as a bird.

"The wizard must have cast a spell," cried the man. His wife fell into his arms weeping, and nothing could console her.

Imagine how confused the boy must have been, suddenly finding himself in the body of a bird, irresistibly flying into the dark forest. Before long, he arrived at the wizard's hut, where he was, just as suddenly, turned back into a boy.

"Ah! There you are," said the wizard. "I have been waiting for you." He led the astonished boy into the small hut that contained the large palace. Then the wizard told the boy about the bargain he had made with his father ten years earlier. "And now you are my apprentice," he said. "I will teach you all that I know." What he did not tell the boy was that he planned to make him his slave.

The boy knew very well that he couldn't escape the wizard's power, no matter how much he longed to return home. So he settled down to his studies, even though it meant learning the black arts—a kind of magic that he would rather not know. He studied day and night, and in a year's time he possessed almost as much power as his master.

In the meantime, his parents had been counting the days. When at last the year was up, the father hurried down the forest path. The wizard glanced into the magic mirror and saw who was coming. He quickly turned the boy back into a bird, and he did the same to two frogs croaking nearby. Now three birds were flying around the palatial chamber.

When the father arrived, the wizard said, "You did not bring your son to me as you promised, even though you knew this would make it hard for you to get him back."

What could the father say? He knew it was his fault, but he pleaded with the wizard, telling him how much he and his wife missed their son.

"Don't you think that *I* would miss him if he left?" asked the wizard.

By now the man was ready to beg for mercy.

"No need for that," the wizard said. "I'll give you a chance. If you can tell me which of these three birds is your son, you may have him back. If not, he will be mine forever."

The man started trembling. If he chose the wrong bird, he would lose his son. He looked them over. All three were identical—black all over. He didn't know what to do.

The bird-boy desperately wanted to send a signal to its father. So it plucked a feather from its tail and held it in its beak. Then, using magic learned from the wizard, it pronounced a spell that turned the feather red. The father spotted it before the wizard could turn it black again. He pointed at the bird-boy. "That's him!" he shouted.

The wizard was furious. He angrily turned the bird back into the boy. Then he grasped his shoulders painfully hard. "You won this time," he said, spitting out his words. "But never again use the magic I taught you, or you will be my slave for the rest of your life."

The moment the wizard let go of the boy, he and his father rushed out the door and down the forest path. They arrived home panting but giddy with happiness. They danced around the room with the boy's mother and vowed they would never be parted again.

But, alas, times grew hard for the family. When all they had left to eat were a few crusts of bread, the boy suggested they use his magic.

"And take the chance of losing you to the wizard?" cried his father.

"How will he know?" asked the boy. "Listen. I'll turn myself into a magnificent horse for you to sell in the marketplace. After the buyer takes me to his stable, I'll wait until everyone is asleep, then I'll turn myself back into a boy and run home."

The father wondered if the evil wizard still had power over the boy's mind. "That is trickery," he said.

"Even if we pay the buyer back?" the boy asked. "As soon as times are better?"

The father didn't like the plan one bit. If there had

been any other way to keep his family from starving, he never would have agreed. But when they had eaten their last crust of bread, the boy turned himself into a horse and his father led it to the marketplace.

And who was watching in his magic mirror? The wizard. He quickly made himself look like a wealthy merchant and sped to the marketplace, where he bought the magnificent horse with a bagful of coins.

Then the disguised wizard jumped onto the horse's back and tugged at the reins, guiding the horse down the forest path to the place where it forked. The horse didn't grow suspicious until it was urged to the right. To the right? That was the way to the wizard's hut.

The horse balked. It realized that the man on its back must be the wizard—so it bucked and threw him to the ground. But the wizard jumped up and said a spell to keep the horse from galloping away. Then he turned a branch into a whip and began to lash the horse unmercifully.

The wizard thought he could easily turn the boy into his slave. But his student had learned too much magic. In a flash, the horse became a boy again—only to be turned back into a horse by the wizard, who lashed it over and over. The horse reared up and then came down hard, stamping a hoof right on the wizard's foot. The man grabbed his foot and shrieked. Then the horse turned itself into a boy and turned the whip into a poisonous snake. Before the wizard could collect his wits, the snake had embedded its fangs in his neck. He howled in pain and fell down—dead.

The boy quickly turned the snake back into a whip and snapped it over the wizard's corpse. A swirl of sulfurous smoke rose into the air and the body vanished.

For the first time since the boy had met the wizard, his mind was completely his own. The whole countryside seemed safe from evil powers.

Or was it? The wizard's hut disappeared. But deep in some forest, somewhere, a swirl of vile smoke hovers over a magic mirror. Who knows what *that* foretells?

SOURCES

A STORY TO TELL

From *Fairy and Folk Tales of the Irish Peasantry*, edited and selected by W. B. Yeats (London and New York: Walter Scott, 1888), pp. 90–93.

COURTING ASTRIAH

From *Sefer Hasidim* (The Book of the Pious), attributed to Rabbi Judah the Pious. Parma edition, Hebrew manuscript de Rossi 33 (Berlin: Yehuda Wistynezki, 1891).

THE SHAGGY GRAY ARM

From *Icelandic Legends*, by Jon Arnason, translated by George E. J. Powell and Eirikur Magnusson (London: Richard Bentley, 1864), pp. 226–28.

THE PRINCE'S FATE
From the Harris Papyrus (No. 500) in the British Museum, about 1300 B.C. Published in *Egyptian Tales*, edited by W. M. Flinders Petrie (London: Methuen & Co. Ltd., 1895; reprint, Mineola, N.Y.: Dover Publications, 1999), pp. 79–87.

THE HEADLESS HORSEMAN
From *Fairy Tales and Traditions of the South of Ireland*, by T. Crofton Croker (London: Murray, 1825), pp. 138–52.

THE KNIFE
From *Sefer Hasidim* (The Book of the Pious), attributed to Rabbi Judah the Pious. Parma edition, Hebrew manuscript de Rossi 33 (Berlin: Yehuda Wistynezki, 1891).

THE WEREWOLF IN THE FOREST
From *Maaseh Buch* (The Book of Tales) (Wilmersdorf and Rodelheim, 1752).

THE SECRET
From *Legends of Florence*, retold by Charles Godfrey Leland (New York: Macmillan and Company, 1895), pp. 114–17.

THE SEVERED HEAD
From *The Book of the Thousand Nights and a Night*, translated from the Arabic by Sir Richard F. Burton,

reprinted from the original edition and edited by Leonard C. Smithers (London: H. S. Nichols & Company, 1897), vol. 1, pp. 41–55.

THE DANGEROUS DEAD

From *Strange Stories from a Chinese Studio,* by P'u Sung-ling, completed in 1679, translated by Herbert A. Giles (New York: Paragon Book Gallery Publishers, 1908), pp. 378–80.

THE HAUNTED BELL

From *Round a Posada Fire: Spanish Legends*, by Mrs. S. G. C. Middlemore (London: W. Satchell and Co., 1881), pp. 126–46.

THE GRUESOME TEST

From *Glimpses of Unfamiliar Japan,* by Lafcadio Hearn (Boston and New York: Houghton Mifflin, 1894), vol. 2, pp. 648–50.

THE ENCHANTED CAVE

From *The Alhambra,* by Washington Irving (Paris: Baudry, 1834), pp. 251–78.

THE WITCH OF THE WOODS

From *Nifla'ot ha-Tzaddikim* (The Wonders of the Righteous) (Piorkow: 1911).

WISHES GONE AWRY
From *Scenes and Legends of the North of Scotland,* by Hugh Miller, edited by Dr. James Robertson (1835; reprint Edinburgh: B & W Publishing, 1994), pp. 278–90.

THE GHOST OF THE RAINBOW MAIDEN
From *Legends of Ghosts and Ghost-Gods,* collected and translated from the Hawaiian by William D. Westervelt (Boston: Ellis Press, 1916), pp. 86–94.

THE WIFE'S TALE
From *Strange Stories from a Chinese Studio,* by P'u Sung-ling, completed in 1679, translated by Herbert A. Giles (New York: Paragon Book Gallery Publishers, 1908), pp. 217–23.

YOUTH WITHOUT AGE
From *Turkish Fairy Tales and Folktales,* by Dr. Ignacz Kunos, translated from the Hungarian by R. Nisbet Bain (London: A. H. Bullen, 1901), pp. 260–75.

THE HAUNTED VIOLIN
From *Sefer Hasidim* (The Book of the Pious), attributed to Rabbi Judah the Pious. Parma edition, Hebrew manuscript de Rossi 33 (Berlin: Yehuda Wistynezki, 1891).

THE EVIL SEA GHOST

From *Trold* *(Trolls)* by Jonas Lie (Copenhagen: Gyldendal, 1891) as found in *Samlede Digterverker* *(Collected Works)* of Jonas Lie, Vol. VIII (Kristiania and Copenhagen: Gyldendal, 1921), pp. 16–25. Translation by James Skurdall.

THE PEASANTS' REVENGE

From *Folk Tales from Many Lands*, retold by Lilian Gask (New York: T. Y. Crowell & Company, 1910), pp. 186–92.

THE WIZARD'S APPRENTICE

From *Yiddishe Folkmayses* (Yiddish Folktales), edited by Yehuda L. Cahan (Vilna: Farlag Yidishe Folklor-Bibliotek, 1931). Told by Moshe Zimnick, who heard it from his grandfather in Belz. A Yiddish variant from Bessarabia is found in "Marchen und Schwanke," collected by Leo Wiener, in *Mitteilugen zur judischen Volkstunde*, vol. 10, no. 2 (1902), pp. 104–07. An oral variant is Israel Folktale Archives 6849, collected by Dov Noy from Isaac Auzon of Morocco.

ARIELLE NORTH OLSON and her coauthor, Howard Schwartz, wrote *Ask the Bones* (Viking), winner of Pennsylvania's Keystone Young Adult Book Award. She has also written three picture books: *Hurry Home, Grandma!*, *The Lighthouse Keeper's Daughter*, and *Noah's Cats and the Devil's Fire*. For twenty-six years, she reviewed children's books for the *St. Louis Post-Dispatch*. Ms. Olson lives in Webster Groves, Missouri, and in Oceanside, Oregon, with her husband, Clarence Olson. They have three children—Randy, Christy, and Jens—and seven grandchildren—Caity, Lindsey, Ian, Rose, Laura, Eric, and Miranda.

HOWARD SCHWARTZ, a noted folklorist, is the author of ten children's books, including *The Diamond Tree*, *Next Year in Jerusalem*, *The Day the Rabbi Disappeared*, and *Before You Were Born*. His books have won many awards, including the National Jewish Book Award, the Aesop Award of the American Folklore Society, the Sydney Taylor Book Award, and the Koret Prize. He teaches at the University of Missouri in St. Louis, where he lives with his wife, Tsila, a calligrapher. They have three children—Shira, Nati, and Miriam—and two grandchildren—Ari and Ava.

E. M. GIST has been a working professional artist since 1998. He began his career designing video games for Gratuitous Games and is now an art teacher at Watts Atelier of the Arts. Gist lives in San Diego, California, with his wife and muse and their dogs.